Finally, she came to the door of the front bedroom. Casey pushed it open and gasped.

There was someone in the room, a dark figure haloed in light. The thought that flashed through Casey's mind was that she'd seen a dark angel.

As Casey scrambled backward, the figure did, too. Suddenly, she realized she was looking at her own reflection in a mirror above the dressing table. Sunlight streaming in from the window behind her had given the impression of a halo.

She slowly stepped toward the mirror. Something about it had caught her eye. She looked closer. The glass surface was covered in dust. Scratched across it, as if someone had traced a finger through it, were two words:

GET OUT

POISON APPLE BOOKS

THE DEAD END

by Mimi McCoy

SCHOLASTIC INC.

New York   Toronto   London   Auckland
Sydney   Mexico City   New Delhi   Hong Kong

No part of this publication may be reproduced, stored in a retrieval system, or transmitted in any form or by any means, electronic, mechanical, photocopying, recording, or otherwise, without written permission of the publisher. For information regarding permission, write to Scholastic Inc., Attention: Permissions Department, 557 Broadway, New York, NY 10012.

ISBN 978-0-545-20318-0

12 11 10 9 8 7 6 5 4   11 12 13 14 15/0

Printed in the U.S.A.   40
First printing, May 2010

For Amanda, with thanks

CHAPTER ONE

"It's the scariest story ever," Casey Slater said in a voice barely above a whisper.

She leaned back on the pillows on her best friend Jillian Morton's bed, holding a fuzzy plush pig in her hands. As she spoke, Casey squeezed the pig tightly.

"Tell me," said Jillian, frowning down at her nails. She was sitting cross-legged on her white bedroom carpet, painting her fingernails traffic-cone orange. The two friends were hanging out in the apartment where Jillian lived with her parents and brother, catching up on gossip from school that afternoon.

Casey shook her head. "I don't even want to say it out loud."

This time Jillian looked up. "Casey," she said with exasperation.

"What?" Casey's large brown eyes widened innocently.

"You always do that. You always say, 'It's the scariest thing ever,' and then you won't say what it is."

"Well, this is really scary," Casey told her.

"Just tell me!"

"Okay. But you asked for it." Casey took a deep breath. "Today I was checking my e-mail during library time. Jaycee Woodard sent me a story about this girl in New Jersey who got *killed*."

"Killed how?" asked Jillian, as Casey knew she would.

"Some girls at her school were teasing her," Casey explained, "and they pushed her down a manhole into the sewer —"

"They pushed her into a *sewer*?" Jillian interrupted. "That's not teasing. That's, like, seriously warped."

Casey raised her eyebrows as if to say, *Do you want to hear the story or what?*

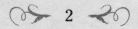

"Sorry," said Jillian. "Go on."

"Well, she never came up," Casey said in a hushed voice. "So the police went down into the sewer and they found her body. She broke her neck when she fell. When the police talked to the girls that pushed her, they all lied and said that she'd fallen by accident, and everybody believed them."

"Wow, that's really horrible," Jillian said.

"I know. But that's not all," Casey told her. "There was another part." This was where the story started to get scary. She gave the plush pig another comforting squeeze.

"The e-mail said to forward it after you read it, so that everybody knows what really happened to the girl," Casey explained. "But a boy who was a friend of Jaycee's cousin didn't forward it. That night when he was taking a shower, he heard this creepy laughter. Well, as soon as he got out of the shower, he ran over to his computer and forwarded the e-mail, but by then it was too late. The next morning the police found him *dead* in the *sewer.*" Casey shuddered. "And when they did the ontopsy —"

"Autopsy," said Jillian.

Casey blinked. "What?"

"When they cut the dead person open," said Jillian, who liked gory TV shows. "It's called an *au*topsy."

"Okay, autopsy. Whatever." Casey felt slightly annoyed at being interrupted during the scariest part. "They found out his neck had been broken in the *exact same place* as the girl who got pushed. And at the bottom of the e-mail it said you have to forward it to five people with the message 'She was pushed!' or you'll wake up in the sewer in the dark, and the ghost of the girl will come get you." Casey gave the pig an extra-hard squeeze.

But Jillian didn't look frightened at all. "Please tell me you did not forward that e-mail," she said, giving her friend a stern look.

"Of course I did!" Casey exclaimed.

Jillian rolled her eyes. "Casey, that story was obviously bogus. People make up that junk just to get you to forward it. It probably had a virus attached."

Casey tried to remember if there had been an attachment. "I don't think so," she said without much confidence.

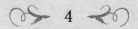

With a jingle of bracelets, Casey pushed her long black bangs out of her eyes and sighed, wondering what she should have done. Which was worse, a computer virus or a killer ghost? It seemed like you were taking your chances big-time either way.

It just reinforced Casey's belief that the world was full of hidden perils. Despite what people said, she thought that what you didn't know probably *would* kill you in the end. It simply did not pay to take chances.

Jillian was the opposite of Casey. She took chances all the time. She Rollerbladed and ate sushi and shopped at secondhand stores. Even Jillian's hair was daring, cut in a sharply angled bob with a long, bleached streak through her bangs. Jillian had gotten the streak after school one day; she'd just walked right into a salon and sat down in the chair like it was something she did all the time. Even though her parents hated the way it looked, there was nothing they could do, Jillian said, because, after all, it was Jillian's hair.

Jillian had encouraged Casey to get a streak, too. But Casey had worried that a bleached stripe in her black hair might make her look like a skunk. Besides, she'd heard that you could get cancer from the peroxide.

"I don't know why you'd pay attention to anything Jaycee Woodard says, anyway," Jillian remarked as she twisted the cap onto the nail polish bottle. "She's so full of it. Remember when she told everyone at school that you can die from swallowing your gum? Which, by the way, you can't. I looked it up."

"But this was her *cousin's friend*," argued Casey, who never swallowed her gum. "So she would know if it was true, right? It's so awful to think that could have happened to someone we almost sort of know."

Casey could clearly picture the boy waking up in the dark sewer, frightened and confused. And somewhere nearby in the shadows, a vengeful ghost lurked, ready to —

"Stop thinking about it," Jillian commanded, pointing an orange fingertip at Casey's nose. "I know you are going to obsess about this. So just stop right now."

Jillian was right. Stories like this always got stuck in Casey's brain. She couldn't forget them even if she wanted to. They were a little like having canker sores. She poked and poked at them, even though she knew it would just make it worse.

"I can't help it," she told Jillian. "It's just so . . . *horrible.*"

"What's horrible," said Jillian, "is that you're killing my pig!"

Casey looked down. She was squeezing the pig so tightly that she looked like she was trying to strangle it.

Casey laughed and threw the pig lightly at Jillian's head. Jillian grinned and ducked. That was the great thing about Jillian. She could always make Casey laugh and forget about whatever was bothering her.

"Let's talk about what we're going to wear to Makayla's party," Jillian said, changing the subject. Makayla Meyers, one of their classmates at James J. Walker Junior High, was having a party the first weekend of summer. Everyone at school had been talking about it.

"You have to see this dress I want to get," Jillian said. She got up and went over to her computer. Very carefully, so as not to disturb her still-drying nails, she typed in an address.

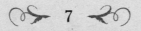 7

Casey got off the bed and went to peer over her shoulder. "Wow," she said, looking at the dress Jillian had pulled up on-screen. It was a green plaid with a smocked top and a tied halter neck; Casey thought it looked like a cross between a swimsuit and a kilt. "Does it, um, come in any other colors?"

"Nope, that's the only one," said Jillian, not taking the hint. "Isn't it cute?"

"Sure," Casey lied. It wasn't worth the trouble to disagree about a dress.

"So what are you wearing?" Jillian asked, swinging around to face Casey.

"I was thinking of just wearing jeans and my coral vest," Casey said.

Jillian shook her head. "Too safe."

"What's wrong with safe?" Casey argued. "Just because I've worn it before doesn't mean it's boring."

Jillian rolled her eyes. "Not 'safe' as in 'boring.' I meant 'safe' as in 'that vest makes you look like a crossing guard.' This is the time for something new and exciting. May I remind you that this party is the first weekend of the first summer . . ."

"Of the rest of our lives," Casey chimed in with a grin. She and Jillian already had their whole summer planned out. "We're going to hang out every single day."

"And we'll meet two cute boys," Jillian reminded her.

Casey nodded. "Who are best friends, too."

"And they'll be our boyfriends. The four of us will do everything together."

"Like, go to the beach . . ."

"And to Six Flags . . ."

"But not on the roller coaster," Casey put in quickly. "I don't do roller coasters."

"Okay," Jillian said with a shrug. "Me and *my* guy will go on the roller coaster, and you and *your* guy can hang out on the merry-go-round or whatever. Either way, it's still going to be the awesomest summer ever."

Casey's cell phone rang. She pulled it out of her pocket and looked at the number. "It's my mom. She's probably calling to tell me to come home for dinner."

"Ask her if you can eat here," Jillian said.

Casey flipped open her phone. "Hi. Can I stay at Jillian's for dinner?" she said.

"Is that how you're answering the phone these days?" her mother replied.

9

Casey sighed. "Hi, *Mom*," she said. "So can I?"

"Not tonight, Casey," Mrs. Slater said. "Dad and I have some news. We'll tell you at dinner. Fifteen minutes, okay?"

"Okay."

"What did she say?" Jillian asked as Casey hung up.

"She said I have to come home. My parents have some kind of big news they want to tell me."

"You better watch out," Jillian warned her. "That's what *my* parents said when they told me we were getting the Pest." The Pest was Jillian's five-year-old brother. She called him that because he was always getting into her stuff and driving her crazy.

Casey picked her backpack up from Jillian's floor and swung it onto her shoulder.

"Call me later," Jillian said.

"I will." The two friends hugged like they always did, then Casey headed for the door.

Outside Jillian's apartment, she took the stairs five flights down to the first floor. Casey tried never to take the elevator, ever since she'd heard a news story about a cable that snapped and sent four people plunging to their doom. There were lots of things that Casey was afraid of, but falling to her death definitely made the top of the list.

Casey and Jillian lived in identical redbrick buildings just two blocks away from each other on the east side of Manhattan. Casey walked slowly, enjoying the early evening. The trees overhanging the sidewalk were thick with leaves, and the warm air felt rich with the promise of the summer ahead. Even the rush-hour crowd, with their briefcases and business suits, seemed to be dawdling more than usual.

As she walked, Casey tried to guess what her parents' news could be. She didn't think it was very likely that they were having a baby; there wasn't room for another person in their small two-bedroom apartment.

Maybe Mom lost her job, Casey thought with a lurch of fear. *Or maybe Dad got fired from the school where he works. And then we'll have to go on welfare, and we probably won't be able to afford our apartment anymore. We'll move to a different part of the city, and I'll have to go to a new school, where the kids are mean and push people into sewers. . . .*

"Stop it," she told herself, interrupting that train of thought. "It's probably nothing like that at all."

Casey sighed. She wished her mother could have just told her the news on the phone. She hated surprises, even good ones.

As she turned onto her block, Casey noticed part of the street was marked off with orange cones. Two workers in blue hard hats were working in an open manhole.

Casey shivered, thinking again of the ghost in the sewer. Tightening her grip on her backpack, she ran the rest of the way home.

CHAPTER TWO

"Hi, Mom! Hi, Dad!" Casey yelled as she came in the door.

The smell of frying meat greeted her. In the tiny entranceway, Casey threw down her backpack and slipped off her sneakers, then headed into the kitchen.

Both her parents were crowded into the narrow space. "Hi, sweetie," said her mother, who was tearing up lettuce for a salad. "Go ahead and wash up. Dinner is almost ready."

Casey squeezed between them to get to the kitchen sink. As she rubbed soap over her hands, she studied her parents, looking for some clue to their big news. Her mother was still dressed in her office clothes, a tan skirt, white blouse, and pumps, her long black hair twisted up in a clip.

She looks tired, Casey thought. But after scrutinizing her mother's face, Casey decided she looked no more tired than usual.

Casey turned her attention to her dad, who was flipping chops in a pan on the stove. She thought she detected some new flecks of gray in his ginger-colored hair, but she couldn't say for sure.

When they were all seated around the table, Casey's dad served up pork chops and salad, while Casey's mom poured iced tea. Finally, Casey couldn't take it any longer.

"So what's the big news?" she asked.

Her parents glanced at each other with secretive smiles. Casey's mother gave a little nod as if to say, *You tell her.*

"We bought a house!" Casey's father said, beaming.

"A house?" Casey's brow wrinkled in confusion. Nobody in Manhattan lived in houses, except for extremely rich people, which the Slaters definitely weren't. "You mean a new apartment?" she asked.

Her dad laughed. "No, Casey. A summerhouse. In New Hampshire. A place where we can really get away from it all."

A house, so that was all. Casey sighed in relief. "So that's where we're going for vacation?" she asked, cutting into her pork chop.

"Even better," her mother replied. "We're going to spend the whole summer there."

"The whole summer?" Casey abruptly put down her knife.

Her mother nodded. "We'll leave the day after school gets out and come back in August."

As the words sank in, Casey felt a cold pit in her stomach. All her beautiful summer plans seemed to dissolve before her eyes.

"This cannot be happening," she murmured. Casey closed her eyes and clenched her hands into tight fists, digging her fingernails into her palms. Whenever she had a nightmare, this was how she woke herself up. The sharp pinch of her nails always jarred her back into reality. Now she squeezed until there were half-moon circles in her skin, but when she opened her eyes, she hadn't moved. She was still sitting at the dinner table. Her parents were both looking at her.

"Casey, are you listening?" her father asked.

Casey let her hands fall to her sides. It was no use. This wasn't a bad dream.

"It's a beautiful old house," her dad went on, "just a few miles from a lake where we can go fishing and picnicking. . . . Maybe I'll even get a boat!" He smiled to himself at the thought.

Fishing? Casey stared at him. The closest her dad had ever come to fishing was opening a can of sardines. She waited for him to say he was kidding, but he was lost in his daydream and didn't seem to notice.

Casey turned to her mother. "*Where* is this house exactly?"

"The town of Stillness. Stillness, New Hampshire — doesn't that sound peaceful? Just wait till you see the place, Casey," her mother replied. "It's a great big old farmhouse with a porch swing. We'll sit out there and drink lemonade and listen to the birds." Her eyes glazed over dreamily.

Casey looked back and forth between her

starry-eyed parents. "But what about your jobs? You can't just leave them!"

"Dad decided not to teach summer school this year," said her mother. "And I'm taking a leave of absence. I have a lot of vacation saved up, and I've worked it out so I can take a few weeks of unpaid leave."

"The house needs some work," her father added. "Fixing it up is going to be our full-time job this summer."

Casey stared at her dinner without really seeing it. "I can't believe you bought a house — a whole entire *house* — without telling me."

"We wanted to surprise you," her father said. "We've always wanted a house in the country. We just never thought we'd be able to afford it. We couldn't believe the asking price on this one, and then the sellers accepted our offer so quickly — it was too good an opportunity to pass up."

"You'll see, sweetie. You'll love it there. Remember how much you enjoyed that time we stayed at the lake in upstate New York?" her mother added.

"That was a *week*. Not a *whole summer*." Casey couldn't let her parents do this to her. Not after everything she and Jillian had planned. There had to be a way out of this!

"I could stay here," Casey said suddenly, thinking out loud. "I could stay with Jillian, while you go to New Hampshire."

Her parents were frowning before she'd even finished the sentence. "Of course you can't stay here, Casey. Don't be silly," said her mom. "We could never ask the Mortons to look after you all summer."

"But it's not fair!" Casey said. She hardly ever talked back to her parents, but this was simply too much to bear. "Did you ever stop to think that maybe I already had plans for this summer?"

"Plans?" her father scoffed. "For heaven's sake, Casey, you're twelve years old."

"I'll be thirteen in August," Casey shot back. "And I did have plans. Jillian and I were going to do all kinds of stuff this summer — which I could have told you about if you'd bothered to ask!"

"Jillian can come up and visit you," Mrs. Slater said reasonably. "It's not that far from New York."

"I don't *want* Jillian to come visit me," Casey said, her voice rising. "I want to stay here!"

"Casey, that's *enough*," her father said sternly. "We're not talking about this any more until you calm down. Now, finish your dinner."

"I'm not hungry." Scraping her chair back, Casey stood up and stalked to her room, slamming the door behind her. It didn't do much good. Casey's bedroom was right next to the kitchen. She heard her dad ask her mom to pass the salad, and the clink of their silverware against their plates. They might as well have been in the same room.

Casey flopped onto her bed, and stared up at the ceiling. She could hear people walking across the floor in the apartment above them. In just a few weeks, she would be in a new room in a house in New Hampshire. Casey tried to imagine it, but all she could picture was the hotel room where they'd stayed by the lake upstate. The carpet had smelled funny, and the toilet had run all night.

Either way, it's still going to be the awesomest summer ever. . . . Jillian's words rang in Casey's ears. She thought about all their plans — the party, the beach, their first-ever boyfriends. None of that could happen now. This was supposed to be the best summer of Casey's life.

And now it was ruined. All because her parents had to go and buy some stupid house.

With a sigh, Casey picked up her cell phone and dialed Jillian to give her the bad news.

CHAPTER THREE

Casey slouched far down in the front seat of the car. Her thumbs flew as she tapped out a message on her cell phone keypad.

911! kidnapped by evil parents. headed 4 nh. send help!

Jillian's reply came back a moment later. can't. lotfcnabchbcurg!

Huh? Casey thought. Usually she could guess Jillian's crazy text abbreviations, but this one was beyond her. ??? she typed.

lying on the floor curled in a ball crying hysterically b/c u r gone! Jillian wrote back.

Casey smiled and typed a quick reply. But when she pressed SEND the message wouldn't go through.

Casey squinted at the screen and groaned. "I lost the signal."

Her mother glanced over from the driver's seat. "Honey, put that thing away," she said unsympathetically. "You're missing the beautiful scenery."

Casey snapped her phone shut and stared gloomily out the window. *What beautiful scenery?* she thought. There was nothing but trees and more trees. It had been like that for miles.

They passed some cows grazing in a field. Casey eyed them apprehensively. She hoped there weren't any animals where they were headed. Animals were unpredictable. Even the pigeons in New York freaked Casey out a little.

They had left New York late that morning, Casey and her mother driving in their little sedan, while Casey's father followed behind in a rented van. Her parents said the house was furnished, but they'd still managed to fill an entire van with things they'd need for the summer: sheets and towels, pots and pans, the stereo and television, tools, toiletries, kitchen appliances, bikes, and at the last minute, a giant inflatable inner tube her father had picked up at the store.

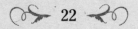

During the first few hours of the trip, Casey recognized towns they'd visited on day trips out of the city. But after they turned off the interstate, the landscape became unfamiliar. The cities and rest stops had given way to green rolling hills and patches of dense forest. It had been several miles since they'd gone through a village. The last building Casey had seen was an abandoned gas station with the ominous sign MILES FROM NOWHERE.

Casey's mother drove with the windows rolled down and her hair whipping in the breeze. When a song she liked came on the radio, she turned up the volume and sang along. Finally, Casey put on her headphones and cranked up her favorite band, No Tomorrow. The gloomy music matched her mood perfectly.

Casey had listened to almost the whole album when they came to a T in the road. A sign pointing to the left read STILLNESS: 1.5 MILES. Casey's mother turned right.

Casey pulled off her headphones. "The sign said Stillness is that way," she said, pointing behind them.

"The house is just outside town," her mother

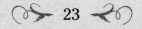

replied. "Our turnoff should be somewhere around here."

A moment later, she turned onto a narrow lane marked Drury Road. *More like* Dreary *Road,* Casey thought, eyeing the shadowy woods that spread out on either side of it.

After a short distance, the pavement ended, and they continued on dirt. Here and there, mailboxes sprouted along the side of the road like tall mushrooms. Casey could see the houses they belonged to hidden back among the trees. She glanced at the side mirror. The van had fallen out of sight.

"Are you sure this is the right way?" she asked her mom.

Mrs. Slater glanced down at the hand-drawn map in her lap. "Pretty sure," she replied, sounding not very sure at all.

When they came to a yellow sign that read DEAD END, Casey was certain they would turn around. To her surprise, her mother sped up.

"This is it!" Mrs. Slater declared confidently.

They followed the lane around a curve and came out of the trees, into a wide patch of overgrown lawn. "We're here!" Casey's mother sang, cutting the engine. "I don't know about you, but I'm ready to stretch my legs."

Casey barely heard her. She was staring at the house that stood before them.

When her parents had mentioned a summer home, Casey had pictured a cozy cottage tucked away among flowering rosebushes. This house was nothing like that. It was tall and narrow and set out in the open. Rows of blank windows stared out beneath a steeply sloping roof. The wood was silver with age, and the front porch railing had two broken slats, like missing teeth. A forest of tall trees pressed up close behind the property.

The house reminded Casey of old bones laid out in the grass to dry. Looking at it, a feeling of desolation swept over her. "I don't want to go in there," she said automatically.

"Casey, don't be silly." Her mother glanced up at the house. "I admit it needs a little work. But that's the beauty of it. We can make it exactly what we want it to be."

She opened the car door and started up to the house, her feet crunching on the gravel drive.

"Aren't you coming?" she called back when Casey didn't move.

Reluctantly, Casey got out of the car and followed her mother up to the porch.

"Just look at that gorgeous period detail!" Mrs. Slater exclaimed, pointing to an oval of glass set into the heavy oak front door. With a jingle of keys, she unlocked the door, and the two of them stepped inside.

It was a hot day, and the air in the house was warm and stale. As her mother bustled about, opening windows, Casey looked around. To the left of the entranceway was a large room with a brick fireplace. Most of the furniture had been covered with white sheets, like hunched and bulky Halloween ghosts. An old-fashioned wooden radio as big as a television set sat in the corner of the room. Casey walked over and twisted the knobs, but it seemed to be broken.

"The furniture is a little outdated," said her mother, briskly whipping back a sheet to reveal an ugly green couch. "But it will do until we find something better."

She led Casey through the next rooms, pointing out the changes she wanted to make. "We'll paint the walls, and refinish the floors. . . . I think we can fit a half bath in that corner. . . ."

Casey nodded, only half listening. The rooms were much bigger than any in their apartment. Yet, strangely, they felt close and suffocating.

"And here," said Casey's mother, stopping in the next doorway, "is the kitchen. Isn't it wonderful?"

Casey's eyes swept over the room. She didn't see what was so great about it. There was a free-standing porcelain sink, a rough wooden table, and an ancient-looking gas stove.

"Are you supposed to cook on that thing or drive it?" Casey asked, eyeing the stove. It had almost as many doors as burners.

"It's a Wedgewood, Casey. An *antique*," her mother replied. "You wouldn't believe how much those things are worth." She looked around and sighed with satisfaction. "The real estate agent said we were lucky to find something so pristine. It's a perfect example of simple country chic."

Casey rolled her eyes. She could tell her mother

was quoting from one of her interior design magazines. Over the last few weeks she'd bought stacks of them. They had littered every room in their apartment, and suddenly, Mrs. Slater was full of ideas about "color palettes" and "interior solutions."

Casey's dad was the same. It seemed like every time she turned around he was nose-deep in a copy of *Do-It-Yourself Doorknobs* or *Learn to Hammer Like a Pro* or some other boring book. It was like both her parents had caught some disease, Casey thought. Some virus that turned them from normal people into home makeover lunatics.

Casey went over to the sink and tried the faucet. It coughed, but no water came out.

"You bought a house without *water*? We're going to die of thirst here!" Casey said, only half joking.

"No one is going to die of thirst, Casey. It's probably just some glitch with the pump." Her mother sighed. "I wish you'd stop sulking and be a little open-minded. I think we're going to have a wonderful summer here."

Fat chance, Casey thought. She figured if she kept sulking long enough, her parents just might take her back to the city.

From outside came the honk of a car horn. Casey and her mother went out to the porch as the van came roaring up in a cloud of dust.

Casey's dad hopped out of the front seat. "Okay, let's start unloading," he said as he swung open the doors to the back. "We've got a lot to get done today."

"Joe, relax," Casey's mom said with a laugh. "We just got here. I haven't even finished showing Casey around."

"There's plenty of time for that later. I don't want to have to pay for an extra day on this van." Casey's father was adamantly against paying extra for anything. "Dez, you come help me. Casey, I want you to start unloading the car."

Dragging her feet, Casey walked over to their Honda and popped open the trunk. It was jammed full of suitcases and bags of things that hadn't made it into the van. She selected the lightest thing she could find — a four-pack of toilet paper — and made a big show of carrying it to the house.

Her dad was wrestling a heavy-looking box. He paused long enough to snap, "Casey, quit messing around."

Apparently, Dad lost his sense of humor somewhere on the drive from New York, Casey thought with a sigh. She trudged back to the car, took out a duffel bag, and lugged it up the porch stairs.

Inside the door, she looked around, wondering where to put it. She was about to take it into the living room, when she heard something overhead. Casey stopped and listened. It sounded like something rolling across the floor.

"Mom?" Casey called, puzzled. She hadn't seen her mother go into the house ahead of her.

"Out here!" Mrs. Slater stuck her head around the side of the moving truck. "What is it?"

"Er . . . nothing," Casey called back.

She looked up toward the ceiling. It was silent now. Setting the duffel bag down against the wall, Casey headed for the stairs, which were off the kitchen.

The staircase was narrow and steep. As she climbed, the wooden steps groaned beneath her feet as if they weren't used to being walked on.

Upstairs it was even hotter. A narrow hallway led from the back of the house to the front, where a tiny sealed window overlooked the front lawn. Casey felt a sudden urge to rush down the stairs and back out into the fresh air. Instead, she pushed open the door to the first room.

It was a small bedroom, furnished simply with a single bed, a wooden chair, and a small dresser with a mirror on top. The walls were covered with fern-patterned paper. There was nothing in it that could have made the sound she'd heard.

Something she'd mistaken for a dust ball suddenly moved across the floor. *Ugh, a spider!* Casey thought with a shiver of disgust. Quickly, she backed out of the room.

The next door led to a simple bathroom with a claw-foot tub. There was nothing in there that could have made the noise either.

Finally, she came to the door of the front bedroom. Casey pushed it open and gasped.

There was someone in the room, a dark figure haloed in light. The thought that flashed through Casey's mind was that she'd seen a dark angel.

As Casey scrambled backward, the figure did, too. Suddenly, she realized she was looking at her own reflection in a mirror above the dressing table.

Sunlight streaming in from the window behind her had given the impression of a halo.

She slowly stepped toward the mirror, and her foot brushed something and sent it skittering across the floor. She bent down to pick it up. It was a marble made of swirled green-and-white glass.

Casey turned the marble over in her hands. It felt solid and heavy. She was sure this was what she had heard rolling across the floor.

But where did it come from? Casey wondered.

As she puzzled over this, Casey caught a glimpse of herself in the mirror. Her wide mouth was turned down at the corners; her dark bangs fell over her furrowed brow. Casey's big brown eyes stared back at her, startled and uncertain.

Casey tucked the marble into her pocket. As she turned to leave, something about the mirror caught her eye. She looked closer. The glass was covered in dust. Scratched into the dust, as if someone had traced a finger through it, were two words.

GET OUT

Casey's heart began to thud. Somebody had been in the house!

From downstairs came a loud thud that made Casey jump.

She hurried to the top of the stairs. What she saw made her heart skip a beat. Her father was sprawled in the entranceway. A large box lay on its side next to him. "Dad!" she cried.

At that moment, Casey's mother came hurrying through the front door. When she saw Casey's father lying on the ground, she gasped. "Joe, what happened? Are you okay?"

Mr. Slater sat up and grimaced. He pointed at the duffel bag Casey had carried in. "Casey left a bag right in front of the door. I tripped over it and just about broke my neck."

"I didn't leave it in front of the door," Casey said. She clearly remembered placing the bag against the wall, where it would be out of the way.

Her father scowled, obviously not believing her. "You need to start helping out here," he growled. "We've got enough to do without you getting in the way."

The tension Casey had felt since they had arrived at the house suddenly burst like a dam. Tears of frustration flooded her eyes. Why was she getting blamed, when it was clear that her dad was the one who'd been clumsy? "Help out here? I don't even want to *be* here!" she exclaimed.

Her dad's face darkened. "Casey —"

Casey's mother put a hand on his arm and gave him a let-me-handle-this look. "Honey, I'm going to drive into town and get something for dinner," she said, turning to Casey. "Why don't you come with me while Dad finishes unloading the van? You want to see what Stillness is like, don't you?"

What I want *is to go home,* Casey thought furiously. But where was home? Their apartment had already been sublet for the summer. This was Casey's home — at least for the next three months.

"Okay." With a resigned sigh, Casey went downstairs and followed her mother out to the car.

Casey's mother had said they were driving to town, but Stillness turned out to be nothing more than a T in the road. There wasn't even a stoplight. On one corner, there was a two-pump gas station attached to a small diner. Across the road sat a trailer that seemed to serve fast food, although it was closed when they drove by. Scattered along the road were a few other storefronts, including a taxidermist, a hardware store, and a hair salon named Sandee's Snip 'n' Clip.

Casey's mother seemed blissfully unaware of her dismal surroundings. "I can't wait to get some local vegetables," she said cheerily. "Maybe some eggs, too. Just wait until you taste eggs that have come straight off a farm, Casey. You'll think you've died and gone to heaven."

They reached the end of Main Street. Beyond that, there were a few houses and fields, then more forest.

"The real estate agent said there was a grocery store right in town. Did you see it?" Mrs. Slater asked. Casey shook her head.

They drove up and down the street a few more times. "I guess we could try in there," Casey said at last. She pointed to a small building next to the gas station. A hand-lettered sign in the window advertised SODA. ICE. WORMS.

Casey's mother parked in front, and they went inside. At the cash register, a teenage girl sat with her chin in her hand, reading a magazine.

"Excuse me," said Mrs. Slater. "Can you tell me where I can find a grocery store around here?"

"You're in it," the girl said. "Unless you mean the Food Mart. That's about twenty minutes down the road."

"Oh . . . er, that's all right. I'm sure we can find something here." Mrs. Slater gazed around at the shelves of dusty-looking canned goods. "Do you have any *fresh* vegetables?"

"Right over there." The girl pointed her chin toward a cooler, where an old man stood examining the expiration date on a carton of milk. Inside the cooler, on a small shelf, there was a wilted head of lettuce, a few pale tomatoes, and some withered apples.

"Wow, Mom. You were right. The local vegetables look *great*," Casey muttered.

Mrs. Slater pursed her lips and frowned. "Casey, go get us some bottled water. I'm going to find something for dinner."

Casey rolled her eyes and shuffled over to the cooler. The old man was still standing in front of it, looking down at the carton in his wrinkled hand.

"Excuse me," Casey said, trying to move past him.

As the man slowly turned his head, his blue eyes widened. He stared at Casey, his mouth open in surprise.

Casey wondered if he was hard of hearing. "Excuse me," she said a little louder. "I just want to get some water." She gestured at the cooler.

At last the man seemed to understand. Slowly, he shuffled out of the way.

"Thanks." Quickly, Casey grabbed three bottles of water and hurried back over to her mom.

"What do you think? Pork and beans or spaghetti and meatballs?" Mrs. Slater asked, holding up two family-sized cans.

"I don't care, Mom. Let's just go," Casey said, tugging at her sleeve. There had been something weird about the way the man had looked at her. *Like he was afraid,* Casey thought.

"Pork and beans it is," said her mother. She picked out a loaf of bread and a couple cans of tuna fish and took them over to the register.

"You know, tuna is on sale. Five cans for four dollars," the girl said.

"I think two is enough," Mrs. Slater said.

"You sure? That's a real good price." She gave

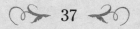

Casey's mother a pointed look. Mrs. Slater sighed, and went to get three more cans.

"You folks headed to the lake?" the girl asked as she rang up their purchases.

"No, we're new in town," Mrs. Slater said. "We just bought the house at the end of Drury Road."

"That place?" The girl stopped ringing up the groceries for a moment to gape at her. "But that house is —"

Smack! A wet splat interrupted her. Everyone turned. The old man had dropped the milk carton he was holding. Milk pooled around his feet, but he didn't seem to notice. He was looking right at Casey. His hands were visibly trembling.

"Oh, Mr. Anderson. You should be more careful," the cashier groaned. She rolled her eyes at Casey's mother and handed over the bag of groceries. "I'd better get a mop. You folks have a good night."

As they walked out of the store, Casey glanced back over her shoulder. The old man was still staring at her.

Outside, the sky had deepened to a bruised purple. "We're going to be eating tuna till it comes out our ears," Casey's mother said as they walked to the car. "Don't worry, sweetie. I'm sure we can find a farm stand somewhere around here."

"What do you think that girl was going to say?" Casey asked. "About the house?"

Her mother shifted the groceries to one hip and dug her keys out of her purse. "Who knows?" she said. "That place has been empty for a while. Maybe she was surprised to hear that someone bought it."

"Oh," Casey said. She got into the car and fastened her seat belt, trying to brush away the thought that was troubling her.

She was almost certain the girl had been about to say that the house was haunted.

CHAPTER FOUR

By the time they got back to Drury Road, most of the light had drained from the sky. The house loomed in the twilight, a deeper blackness in the gathering gloom. The thought of spending the night there made Casey feel uneasy. She wondered why there weren't any lights on.

Her father was standing out on the porch. He had unloaded most of the van; bags and boxes were strewn around the porch. But Mr. Slater wasn't moving anything. He just leaned against the porch railing, his face tilted up to the sky.

"What are you looking at?" Casey's mother asked him as they got out of the car.

He pointed at a pair of dark shapes swooping through the air.

"Swallows?" asked Casey's mom.

Mr. Slater shook his head. "Bats."

"Bats?" squealed Casey. Suddenly, the dark house seemed a lot more inviting. "I'm going inside!"

"I'm right behind you," said her mother.

"They're probably harmless," Casey's father said, but he ducked and waved his arms when one flew too close to his head.

Inside the house, Mrs. Slater flipped the light switch in the front hallway. Nothing happened.

"I already tried that," Casey's father said, coming behind them. He had a flashlight in his hand. "It doesn't work. The electricity probably hasn't been turned on in ages."

As Casey's father led the way down the hall, the flashlight beam picked up glimpses of the house: the foot of the stairs. A cobwebbed corner. The molding around a doorway. Beyond the small circle of light, the darkness seemed vast. Casey walked so close behind her mother that she stepped on her heels.

"Ow. Casey!" Mrs. Slater snapped.

"Sorry," Casey mumbled. But as the circle of light moved ahead she hurried to follow it.

In the kitchen, they discovered that the electricity wasn't the only problem. The old gas stove didn't work either.

"Well, it's too hot to cook, anyway," Casey's mother said with a sigh, looking down at the can of pork and beans she'd been planning to heat. "I'll make some tuna sandwiches, too."

They ate dinner on a blanket spread out in front of the fireplace. "Isn't this fun?" Mrs. Slater said as she lit some candles she'd dug out of a box. "Just like a picnic!"

Casey poked at the cold pork and beans on her plate. *Fun* wasn't exactly the word that sprang to mind.

As she scooped up a spoonful of beans, the candles abruptly went out.

"Oh!" Mrs. Slater exclaimed as the room plunged into darkness. She fumbled for the box of matches and relit them.

But a moment later, the same thing happened. Both candle flames sputtered and suddenly went out. This time one of the candles even toppled and rolled across the floor.

"There must be a draft," Casey's mother said, reaching for the matches again.

"Leave it, Dez," Casey's father replied. "Tomorrow when I drive into town I'll see about the electricity."

They ate in the dark in silence. The cold pork and beans and warm tuna fish made Casey gag. After a few more bites, she pushed her plate away.

"I guess I'm not so hungry," she said. "I think I'll just go to bed. . . ." She broke off, realizing that she didn't know where to sleep.

Suddenly, Casey remembered the message she'd seen on the mirror upstairs. She'd forgotten about it in all the commotion. "I think someone's been in the house," she said.

Both her parents stopped eating. "What do you mean?" asked her mother.

"Earlier this afternoon, when I was upstairs, I saw something written on a mirror in one of the bedrooms."

"You mean graffiti?"

"Not exactly. It was written in the dust."

"What did it say?" her father asked.

Casey swallowed. "'Get out.'"

"It was probably just kids fooling around. The agent said this place was broken into a while back," Casey's dad said. "I'll take a look."

He switched on the flashlight and headed up the stairs. Casey and her mother followed closely behind him.

"It was the last room. At the end of the hall," Casey said.

When they got to the room, Mr. Slater trained the flashlight on the mirror. "You said it was written here?"

"In the dust," Casey told him. She took the flashlight from him, holding it at an angle to the mirror.

"I don't see anything," said her father. "Maybe you imagined it, Casey. It could have been a trick of the light."

"I didn't imagine it," she insisted.

She swept the beam of light over the mirror again, but her dad was right. There was nothing there. The surface had been wiped clean.

CHAPTER FIVE

That night, Casey had trouble sleeping. Her room was stiflingly hot. Casey's parents had given her the small cozy bedroom over the kitchen. With the electricity out, the ceiling fan didn't work, and the single window over Casey's bed was painted shut.

Worse than the heat was the silence. Unlike their Manhattan apartment, where the hum of Second Avenue traffic was a soothing reminder of life outside, the house in Stillness seemed eerily quiet. Every tiny noise was amplified and embellished by Casey's imagination. A rustling in the leaves was an escaped convict. A dog barking in the distance definitely sounded rabid. A thump at the window sent Casey racing to wake up her dad. (An investigation with the flashlight revealed the culprit to be a moth.)

And then there was the wallpaper. During the day, the leafy fern design had seemed soothing and pleasant. But now, in the moonlight, the fronds seemed to twist and writhe, like shriveled hands. A dripping faucet down the hall provided a sinister tempo for Casey's fearful imaginings.

Finally, in the early hours of the morning, she fell into an uneasy sleep.

She dreamed she was playing hide-and-seek in the house. There were other children, too, but Casey couldn't see them from her hiding place. She heard the sound of footsteps coming toward her. And suddenly a voice cried out, *"Ready or not, here I come. . . ."*

Casey started awake. For a moment, she didn't know where she was. Slowly, the darkness around her became the shapes of the curtains, the dresser, the chair. The singsong voice from her dream still rang in Casey's ears, and for a second she wondered if she'd really heard it.

No, Casey thought, coming more awake. *Of course I didn't hear it.* It was the middle of the night. The only people around were her parents, asleep down the hall. She could hear her father snoring.

Casey lay awake for a long time, troubled by something she couldn't name. The sky was starting to turn gray by the time she fell asleep again.

When Casey opened her eyes, her room was bright with sunlight. Outside in the trees, birds trilled and squawked. She guessed it was late morning.

Casey climbed out of bed. She put on the shorts she'd been wearing the day before and a clean T-shirt.

In the kitchen, she found her mother unpacking a box of dishes. Mrs. Slater was wearing a pair of old jeans, and her thick black hair was tied back with a blue bandanna. She looked different than she did in the city, Casey thought. She looked young and happy.

"Good morning, sleepyhead," said her mother. "You're sure up late."

"I didn't sleep very well last night," Casey admitted.

Her mother wiped off a dish and set it in a cupboard. "Well, a new house can take some getting used to. Want some breakfast? A tuna sandwich, maybe?" she joked.

Casey made a face.

"Well, have a slice of bread, then. I'd offer you some butter but I haven't found the butter knives yet." She looked in dismay at the boxes that surrounded her feet.

Casey took a slice of bread from the wrapped loaf. She leaned against the sink, chewing. "Where's Dad?" she asked.

"Getting the last few boxes out of the rental truck. He's going to take it back into town this morning and run a few errands. I'll pick him up in the car later this afternoon."

Casey's dad came striding purposefully into the room. He stopped in the middle of the kitchen and looked around, running his hands through his hair. "Has anyone seen the keys to the van?"

"Where did you leave them?" Casey's mother asked.

"I *thought* I left them on the fireplace mantel. But they're not there. I've looked everywhere."

"Haven't seen them," Casey said.

Mrs. Slater shook her head.

"Hmph," Casey's dad grunted. He strode back out of the room. They could hear him rifling through boxes in the living room.

A few moments later, he reappeared in the door-way of the kitchen, dangling the keys from his fingers. "Found 'em! You'll never believe where they were."

"In your pocket?" Mrs. Slater guessed wryly.

"Nope. Behind the toilet in the bathroom."

"How on earth did they get there?" she asked in surprise.

"I have no idea," Mr. Slater replied, shifting his gaze to Casey.

"Don't look at me!" she said. "What would I want with the van keys?"

"I have no idea," her father replied. "Well, I'm off." He kissed Casey's mom on the cheek. "See you this afternoon."

After he left, Casey's mom turned to her. "I don't feel like unpacking any more this morning.

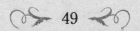

I thought you and I could have some fun exploring the attic."

"There's an attic?" Casey asked.

"Yep, and it's full of stuff. The last owners didn't bother to clean it out. Who knows what we'll find up there?" Mrs. Slater's eyes gleamed.

Casey's mother was a flea-market fanatic. She could spend hours at tag sales and antique shops, sifting through other people's old belongings. Casey knew an attic full of undiscovered junk was like her dream come true.

"Sure," she told her mother with a shrug. "It beats unpacking boxes, anyway."

On her way upstairs, Casey tried to call Jillian, but she still couldn't get a signal. Casey hoped that one of her dad's errands in town was seeing about a phone line for the house.

The stairs to the attic turned out to be at the end of the upstairs hallway, behind a door Casey had mistaken for a closet. As they climbed, the air seemed to get closer with each step. Casey passed the back of her hand across her damp forehead. *This place sure could use some A/C,* she thought.

The stairs led straight up through a hole in the attic floor. "Wow!" Casey said as she climbed into the room. It was nearly as long as the house, and crammed end to end with junk.

Mrs. Slater's face lit up like she'd just won the jackpot. "There must be some real treasures in here!"

"It's stuffy," Casey remarked, fanning herself with a hand. "And hot. I feel like I can't breathe."

"We'll let some air in," Mrs. Slater said. She went to the small, grimy window at one end of the room and tugged it open.

As her mother began sifting through boxes, Casey poked around in an old bureau. The top drawer was filled with handkerchiefs. They all had the letter *H* embroidered in the corner.

Casey plucked one between her fingertips. It was stained and yellowed with age. Quickly, she tossed it back in the drawer, and rubbed her hand against her shorts to get off any germs.

In the next drawer, Casey found a stack of black-and-white photographs. She quickly flipped through them. Most were of the same unsmiling man and woman, taken in different places. Next to an old-fashioned car. At the beach in funny-looking swimsuits. In front of a house, holding the hands of a little girl. Casey looked more closely and realized the house in the background was the farmhouse. It looked different with a fresh coat of white paint and bushes growing out front.

"Casey, look at these."

Her mother was holding out a wooden crate full of books. Casey took it from her and glanced through the titles. They were children's novels for the most part: *Peter Pan*, *The Jungle Book*, *Treasure Island*, as well as some stories she'd never heard of.

Casey picked up one of the books and flipped through it. It had pretty illustrations of fat bluebirds and pink-cheeked boys and girls.

"Now you'll have plenty to read this summer," her mother said, moving off to another corner of the attic.

Casey set the books aside and lifted her hair off the back of her neck. The open window hadn't done much to cool things down, and the heat was oppressive. But that wasn't the only thing that was bothering her. There was something about the attic that made Casey feel nervous and trapped.

"Oh!" Mrs. Slater suddenly exclaimed. "Isn't this a beauty!"

Casey went over to her. In a corner of the attic, her mother had unearthed a huge trunk with a tarnished brass lock and leather handles.

"What is it?" Casey asked.

"An old steamer trunk," her mother replied. "People used them to carry their belongings on long trips, before they had suitcases." She studied the trunk with a practiced eye. "It's unusual to find one in such good condition. I wonder what's in it."

She tried the lid but it didn't budge. "It's stuck. Or locked." Mrs. Slater looked around for something to open it. "I don't see a key."

As Casey looked at the trunk, a wave of apprehension swept over her. "If there's no key, then we can't open it, right? We should just forget it."

"Just a minute. I want to try. There might be something good inside." Mrs. Slater rummaged around and came back with a rusted letter opener.

Casey's terrible feeling grew stronger. As her mother jiggled the opener in the lock, Casey started to panic.

"Don't open it!" she screamed.

Mrs. Slater looked at her, startled. "Casey! What on earth is wrong?"

"I . . . don't know." Casey couldn't explain why she found the trunk so horrifying.

Her mother nudged the lid one last time. "Well, it's not going to budge." She gave Casey a curious look. "You're a little pale. Why don't you take a break, and get some fresh air? I'll finish up and be down soon."

Casey nodded, relieved to get out of the room. As she descended the stairs, she still felt shaky. *What happened in there?* she wondered. She wished she could call Jillian. Her best friend would probably have some funny explanation, and the two of them could laugh about it together.

Despite the hot day, it was cool on the first floor. As Casey stepped into the front hallway, the hairs on her neck prickled. She had a feeling she was being watched.

Casey glanced back over her shoulder. The

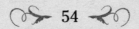

stairway was empty. She looked into the living and dining rooms. They were empty, too.

I'm imagining things, Casey thought. *Mom is right. I do probably need some fresh air.*

She started toward the front door, and froze. There was a face in the glass window. A pale face, staring right at her.

Casey screamed.

CHAPTER SIX

At once, the face disappeared. A second later, Casey heard a thump, followed by a muffled curse. Heart pounding, she went to the front door and yanked it open.

A boy was standing on the porch. He was bent over, grasping his bare toe as if he'd just stubbed it. When he saw Casey he froze, a half-guilty, half-curious expression on his face.

"What are you doing?" Casey exclaimed. She was frightened and her voice came out louder than she'd meant it to.

The boy blinked in surprise and let go of his foot. "I brought some food," he said, pointing to a covered foil pan he'd left in front of the door. "It's from my mom."

When Casey didn't say anything, he added, "We live in the big green house just down the way. I'm Erik Greer."

He was a little bit taller than Casey, with a square chin and light blue-gray eyes. A froth of curly white-blond hair topped his head like a pile of whipped cream.

Casey suddenly thought of the message on the mirror. *Could this boy be the one who wrote it?* she wondered. Maybe the food was just a ruse, and he was actually scouting their house, planning another break-in.

"Why were you looking in our window?" she asked, narrowing her eyes suspiciously.

"I wanted to see if anyone was home," Erik said with a shrug. "I rang the doorbell, but I don't think it works. I didn't mean to scare you." He cocked his head and added, "You sure can scream."

Casey felt herself blush.

"Casey?" Mrs. Slater came to the door behind her. "Oh, hello. I thought I heard voices," she said when she saw Erik. "I'm Desiree Slater. We just moved in."

"Erik Greer," said Erik. "We live just down the road. My mom sent over some supper for you. She would have come herself, but she's too busy with the kids and Gran," he explained.

Mrs. Slater looked down at the covered dish, which was still sitting in front of the door. She picked it up and smiled warmly. "That's very kind. Tell your mother thank you. I look forward to meeting her. And I see you've already met my daughter, Casey."

"Not officially." Erik turned to Casey and raised his eyebrows. "Nice to meet you, Casey."

She didn't say anything. She could tell from his smile that he was teasing her.

"I guess she's scared of me," Erik confided to Casey's mom. "She screamed when I showed up."

"It's not you. It's this peaceful country life," Mrs. Slater replied with a laugh. "It's got Casey on edge."

Casey scowled at her mother. She thought it was rude of them to be talking about her like she wasn't there. She didn't care much for this boy and his smug smile. She hoped he would leave soon.

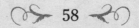

To her dismay, her mother asked, "Can you stay for lunch, Erik?"

Erik took a step backward and shook his head. "I have to get going," he replied, a little too quickly. "Mom says don't worry about returning the dish. See you around," he added to Casey. He turned and headed back down the lane.

"Well, wasn't *he* cute," said Mrs. Slater to Casey.

"Shhh, Mom! He'll hear you," Casey hissed. "Anyway, I didn't think he was so great." But she continued to watch Erik as he disappeared around the bend.

"It was certainly nice of him to bring over lunch," her mother replied. "I'm dying to try some local cuisine."

She eagerly peeled back the foil, and her face fell.

"What's wrong?" asked Casey. "What is it?"

Mrs. Slater sighed. "Tuna casserole."

Later that afternoon, Casey's mother drove to the nearest big town to pick up Casey's dad, since he'd dropped off the van and needed a ride back.

"You can come if you want," she said to Casey. "But I think it might be nice if you spent some time today unpacking your room. I don't want you living out of your suitcase all summer." Her tone made it clear what she wanted Casey to do.

"I guess I'll stay," Casey said.

The instant her mother drove off, Casey regretted her decision. With both her parents gone, the house seemed even gloomier.

Upstairs, Casey slowly unpacked her suitcase, carefully folding each item before placing it in the little chest of drawers. The dresser was full long before her suitcase was empty, and Casey was sorry she'd packed so many clothes. She could already tell that she wasn't going to have much use for her blue satin bubble skirt and her platform sandals in New Hampshire.

Casey shoved the half-full suitcase under her bed, then sat back on her heels, brushing damp tendrils of hair away from her face. Even that small effort had made her sticky with sweat. She lifted the hair off the back of her neck to cool it, staring resentfully up at the motionless ceiling fan.

"What's the point of having an electric fan if

you don't have any electricity?" she grumbled to herself.

By now it was late afternoon. Casey's bedroom had settled into a dusky gloom. She hoped her parents would hurry. Sunset wasn't far off, and she didn't think she'd be able to stand a single second alone in the dark, empty house.

As she got to her feet, she felt a cooling breeze across the back of her neck. Casey looked up and saw the ceiling fan slowly rotating.

"Wha — ?" She glanced toward the windows, thinking a breeze might have stirred it. But both windows were closed.

The fan began to whir faster, lifting strands of her hair. At that moment, the overhead lights came on. The sudden brightness made Casey jump. Somewhere downstairs, she could hear an indistinct murmur.

Her heart leaped into her throat. Were those . . . *voices*?

She held her breath and listened. Yes, it was definitely the sound of people talking, sometimes a single deep man's voice, sometimes several voices at once. Casey couldn't make out what they were saying. The words were indistinct, punctuated by bursts of static. Now and then, she thought she heard faint strains of music.

The fan was now spinning so fast it shook on its base. Suddenly, one of the wooden blades came loose. It sliced through the air and smacked the wall right next to Casey's head. She screamed and ran from the room.

In the hallway, the lights were blazing. Casey could hear fans rattling in the other bedrooms. Downstairs, the noises were growing louder. They were coming from the parlor. Casey stood there, torn between her need to escape and her fear of whatever was down there.

Then she remembered: The kitchen had a back door!

Casey raced down the stairs, skipping steps and stumbling in her haste. The lights in the dining room and kitchen were on as well. From the parlor, there came a burst of music, a jazzy ragtime melody that switched suddenly back to the man's deep voice.

Casey drew up short. She recognized that voice. It belonged to a popular talk-show host.

Switching directions, Casey crept through the

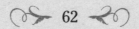

dining room toward the parlor. As with the other rooms, the lights were on and the ceiling fan whirred, but there was no one there. In the corner, the tall wooden radio was on, full blast. It seemed to be tuning in and out of different stations.

As Casey stood there, the lights went out, as abruptly as they'd gone on. The fans slowed to a halt. The radio fell silent. In a few seconds, the house was as dark and quiet as it had been moments before.

Casey let herself out the door with trembling hands. On the porch, she took deep gulps of air and tried to think.

Whenever Casey encountered something suspicious or strange, she always imagined the worst. But now something truly frightening had happened, and she found herself searching for plausible reasons.

"Dad was going to check on the electricity," she told herself. "He probably got it turned on and there was a big power surge and everything came on at once. That's all it was."

She was only the faintest bit reassured. Casey looked out toward the road. She considered running to get one of the neighbors. But the sun had started to go behind the trees. The woods between her and the nearest house were dark with shadows.

And what would I tell them? Casey thought. *That the lights came on and I got scared?*

Too afraid to go back into the house and too afraid to venture beyond it, Casey finally sat down on the porch steps. She was still sitting there half an hour later, when her parents' car appeared around the bend.

Casey leaped up and ran to meet them as the car pulled to a stop. "What took you so long?" she cried.

"We found a wonderful little farm stand off the highway." Casey's mother held up a paper bag full of vegetables. "I'm going to make a big salad for dinner tonight."

"We stopped at the grocery store, too," her dad said, starting to unload bags from the trunk. "Casey, come help me carry these inside."

Casey didn't move. "You went to the electric company, right? You got the electricity turned on?"

"Well, I tried," said her father. "But they said this house doesn't show up on the grid. They're sending someone out tomorrow to make sure we're connected."

"Honey, is something wrong?" her mother asked, noticing Casey's pale face.

"Everything came on," she told them. "Lights, fans, the radio — everything. It all came on at once."

"That's unlikely," said her father. "According to the electric company, we shouldn't have any power."

"But it did," Casey insisted. "My fan was whipping so fast one of the blades came off. It almost hit me in the head!"

With her parents there, she felt enough courage to go back into the house. She led them up to her room and showed them the broken fan.

"It's strange," said her father, turning the blade over in his hands. He flicked the light switch on and off a few times, but nothing happened.

"Maybe the electric company was wrong. It wouldn't be a first." Casey's dad glanced up at the fan. "Those other blades could be loose, too. I'll have to replace the whole thing. This could have taken your eye out," he added, tapping the blade.

Casey shuddered to think how close it had come. "I don't want to sleep in here anymore," she told her parents.

They both frowned. "But where else are you going to sleep?" asked her mother.

"I could . . . sleep in your room. With you guys," Casey suggested. She knew it sounded babyish. But right at that moment, she didn't care.

"Honey, it was just an accident," her mother said, putting an arm around her. Casey knew that the answer was no.

"It's nothing to worry about," Mrs. Slater added. "Dad will get the fan fixed."

"Everything will be fine," Casey's father agreed. "You'll see."

That night after Casey went to bed, her mother came to tuck her in. That afternoon, they had bought some battery-operated lanterns at the store, and now she set one next to Casey's bed.

"Isn't this the sweetest room?" Mrs. Slater sat on the edge of the bed, looking around. Casey could practically see visions of window treatments dancing before her eyes.

"The walls need to be painted, of course," her mother said. "I was thinking a nice cornflower blue with white trim. And we'll get you a pretty bedspread to match. Would you like that?"

"Mmm," said Casey. She didn't care what color they painted the walls. It wouldn't make her feel any better. "Mom, can I ask you something?"

"Sure, honey."

"Do you believe in ghosts?"

"Ghosts?" Mrs. Slater raised her eyebrows. "No, sweetie, not really. Why do you ask?"

"I don't know." Casey shrugged uncomfortably. "It's just . . . this house. It kind of gives me the creeps."

Her mother sighed. "This is a very old house, Casey. It's not like our New York apartment. It's bound to have some little quirks. Don't let that wild imagination of yours get carried away, okay?"

"Okay," Casey said.

"Now, stop all this spooky talk and get some sleep. We have another big day tomorrow." Casey's mother kissed her on the forehead. Then she switched off the lantern and left the room.

Casey lay there in the dark for a moment. Then she reached over and switched the lantern back on. Her mother was probably right. She was probably imagining things.

But it's better to leave the light on, Casey thought. *Just in case.*

CHAPTER SEVEN

The next day, after breakfast, Casey rode her bike into town with a pocketful of quarters. At the gas station, she used the pay phone to call Jillian.

"Omigosh!" Jillian squealed when she picked up. "Girl, where have you been? I've called your cell phone a hundred times! I thought you were dead!"

It was so good to hear Jillian's cheerful voice. Casey tightened her grip on the phone. "I can't get any reception out here," she told her friend. "And we don't have a landline yet. I'm calling you from a pay phone."

"You sound like you're calling from Mars," Jillian said.

"Mars. New Hampshire. Same difference," Casey joked. "Hold on, I think I see a Martian. Do they wear flannel shirts and drive pickup trucks?"

Jillian giggled. "I have so much to tell you," she gushed. "Wait till you hear what happened at Makayla's party!"

Casey leaned against the side of the gas station, as Jillian launched into her story. She carefully described what everyone had worn to the party, and who had been flirting with whom.

"Wow, it sounds fun," Casey said enviously.

"Hold on! I haven't even gotten to the best part," Jillian told her. "You know that guy David, the one in our math class, who —"

"Wait, wait!" Casey interrupted. A recorded voice was telling her, *"Please insert one dollar to continue this call."* She dug the change out of her pocket, and tipped it into the slot. "Okay, go on."

". . . Andrew told Leela that David thought I was cute," continued Jillian, who had never stopped talking. "So when I saw David at the party, I walked over and asked him if he wanted to do something sometime."

The boldness of this nearly knocked the breath

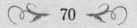

out of Casey. "You mean, you asked him out? Like on a date?"

"Yup," said Jillian.

"What did he say?"

"Duh. He said yes!" Jillian told her. "What did you think? We're going to the movies on Friday, and my mom says it's okay, because we're going in a group. But everybody knows it's a real date."

"Gosh, that's . . . great." Casey tried to swallow around the lump in her throat.

I'm happy for Jillian. I am, she told herself. But part of her felt like crying. Jillian was going to parties and out on dates — all the things they'd planned to do together this summer. Now Jillian was doing them without her.

"Anyway, what's up with you?" Jillian said. "How's your new house?"

"Er . . . it's big." Casey hesitated. She had been planning to tell Jillian about the freaky thing that had happened the day before. But now in the bright daylight, it seemed sort of silly. Casey remembered what Jillian had said about the ghost girl in the sewer. *She'll probably think I'm overreacting,* she thought.

"Have you met any other kids?" Jillian asked her.

"No," said Casey. "I mean — yes. One. This boy named Erik."

"Is he cute?" Jillian asked with interest.

Casey frowned. This conversation wasn't going how she'd imagined. "I don't know," she said. "I guess so. But that's not the —"

"Please insert one dollar to continue this call," the recorded voice broke in again. *"Please insert . . ."*

"Okay, okay." Casey reached into her pocket, but she had used up all her change. "Jillian, I have to go," she tried to shout over the recording. "I'll call you soon. I miss y —"

Click. The line hung up.

Casey reluctantly placed the receiver back on the hook. She lingered near the phone a little longer, hoping that Jillian might try to call back. But the phone didn't ring, and after a while the gas station attendant started to scowl in Casey's direction.

Finally, with a sigh, Casey picked up her bike and pedaled home.

*   *   *

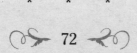

When she got to the house, she saw a strange truck parked in the driveway. Casey dropped her bike by the front porch and went inside.

Her parents were in the kitchen, talking to a man in a matching light blue shirt and cap. The cap read DUSSY ELECTRIC across the front.

"This is your problem," the man was saying. He held up a bit of frayed wire. "The lines connecting to the main fuse box were all worn-out. I went ahead and replaced them, but you may want to think about getting the whole house rewired and putting in a new circuit breaker box."

Casey's dad made a face like he'd tasted something bitter. "How much is that going to cost?"

"It won't be cheap," the electrician said. "But it would be a whole lot safer." He pushed his cap back on his head. "Anyway, at least you'll have some power now."

"But we had it already, right?" Casey spoke up. "It was working yesterday."

The electrician turned to look at her. "It couldn't have been," he said. "The main line was worn completely through. This house hasn't had any power for years."

CHAPTER EIGHT

Casey never found an explanation for the strange surge of electricity. After a while, she managed to push it to the back of her mind.

Time passed, and her days began to fall into a routine. Most mornings, after breakfast, Casey rode her bike into town to call Jillian from the gas station pay phone. (Her parents still hadn't done anything about getting a landline. When Casey pressed them about it, her father just shrugged and said he was glad for the peace and quiet for a change.) More often than not, though, Jillian was too busy to talk for long. She was always heading off to a movie or some event in the park, usually with David. From the sound of it, Casey thought, Jillian *was* having the best summer ever — and she didn't need Casey there to do it.

Casey spent the afternoons roaming the property. The house sat on a half acre of dry, grassy field, bordered by forest. Casey picked clover flowers and tried to weave them into daisy chains. She collected rocks with interesting shapes. She made elaborate snacks from the things her mother picked up at the farm stand: raspberries with maple syrup and burnt-sugar candy; tomato-and-cucumber sandwiches with the crusts cut off. She watched movies on her computer. She listened to music. She painted her nails. In short, she was bored out of her mind.

Her parents knew she was unhappy, but they didn't do anything to help her with it. Her boredom only seemed to irritate them.

"For Pete's sake, Casey, you're old enough to entertain yourself," her dad said when she complained that there was nothing to do. The trip to the nearby lake seemed to have been long forgotten. Her parents spent every spare minute working on the house. Casey's father replaced the fan in her bedroom, patched the porch railing, and tinkered with the old stove until he got it to work. Casey's mother scraped at wallpaper, painted window frames, hung curtains. After a few weeks, the place began to look more lived in. But to Casey it never felt cozy or comfortable, and despite the new curtains and fresh paint, the house never quite lost its air of abandonment.

Nights in the house were the worst. The lights now worked, but they often flickered, sending a flutter through Casey's stomach. Late at night, alone in her room, the darkness seemed to press in close. At those times, Casey's imagination ran wild.

One day, after they had been there for more than three weeks, Casey reached her wit's end. Her parents were upstairs in their bedroom, scraping wallpaper, and Casey wandered through the house, desperately looking for something to do. The blank TV sat against a wall in the parlor, unplugged, since there was no cable. She couldn't text her friends or surf online. Even the battery for her MP3 player was dead.

In a corner of the living room, atop some boxes they hadn't bothered to unpack, Casey discovered the crate full of books her mother had found in the attic. She browsed through it. They were mostly adventure stories, illustrated with pastel scenes of pirate ships and talking animals. Inside the cover of each book, someone had written the letters M.A.H.

Near the bottom of the crate, Casey came across a small red cloth book without a title. On the first page, in uneven, sloping cursive, it read:

MILLICENT AMELIA HUGHES

M.A.H., Casey thought. *Millicent Amelia Hughes. These must be her books.*

She turned the page. *May 26, 1939*, it said at the top. After that was more of the same clumsy hand-writing broken up by dates.

It's a diary, Casey realized. She wondered if she ought to put it away. She'd always been told that it was rude to read someone else's diary.

But Millicent Amelia Hughes obviously doesn't care if someone else reads her diary, Casey reasoned, *or she wouldn't have left it in some dusty old attic for anyone to find.*

Casey got a glass of cold water from the kitchen and took the diary out to the front porch. Settling onto the porch swing, she turned to the first page.

The slanted handwriting was difficult to read. She struggled to make out the first few words. *"Dearest friend . . ."* it began.

CHAPTER NINE

May 26, 1939

Dearest friend,

Mama gave me this diary today. She said I should use it to practice my penmanship. "Your handwriting is as bad as a monkey's," she said. I said, "How do you know? Have you ever seen a monkey's handwriting?" Mama just rolled her eyes to the heavens, as if to say, "Lord, you see what I put up with?"

Mama has been rolling her eyes a lot lately. She rolled her eyes when she caught me chewing tree sap, and when I got my school clothes all muddy by wading in the stream. I heard her tell Papa she's afraid I will become a country bumpkin living here in Stillness. "How will she ever find a good husband?" Mama said.

I don't care a whit about husbands. I want to become a nurse, because I think I would like to take care of people. But if there's one way to get Mama started, it's to tell her that. I'm better off just practicing my handwriting.

We moved to Stillness six months ago for Papa's job at the Stillwater Bank. Before that, we lived in Manchester. Mama always says how lucky we are that Papa found such a good job. But I know she secretly misses the city. When we go to the general store, Mama makes little sighing noises, and I know she is thinking, "The coffee was better in <u>Manchester</u>. The biscuits weren't stale in <u>Manchester</u>."

But I like it here in Stillness. There are lots of trees and pretty flowers and a stream where I can go wading (as long as I don't get my clothes wet). Papa planted an elm tree by our house. He says when it gets big enough he will hang a swing for me. I hope it grows fast! In the meantime, I have to make do with the porch swing.

My cat, Bagheera, likes it here, too. He stalks through the grass, pretending he is a real panther instead of just a silly gray tabby. Today I saw him chasing crickets.

So, I have everything I could wish for here —
almost. I do wish I had a friend. There aren't any girls
my age on Drury Road, only a boy named Gunner
Anderson. He is twelve years old, the same age as me,
but I don't like him. He thinks he is so clever. Oh, and
there is the Swedish family, the Henrikssons. They
have lots of boys and one little girl, Anna. But
they just moved here from Sweden, and I can never
understand what they are saying. Anna is too young to
be my friend, anyway, because she is only six years
old and I am twelve, like I said.

But now, dear diary, you can be my friend. I
will tell you all my secrets, just like I would a real
friend.

Yours truly,
Millie

May 27
Dearest friend,
Today I found a little chickadee that Bagheera had
caught on one of his hunts. It wasn't hurt so far as I
could see, but it was so scared that it didn't even peep
when I picked it up. I could feel its tiny heart beating
fast. I found an old hatbox and made a nest out of

grass and leaves and some petals from Mama's yellow roses. I put the bird inside, and tried to feed it some water from a spoon.

Afterward, I caught Bagheera and gave him a good scolding, but he just flicked his tail and didn't act sorry at all.

When it is better, maybe the bird can be my pet. I will walk around town with a chickadee on my shoulder, like Long John Silver with his parrot. Wouldn't that be funny!

I am now more sure than ever that I want to be a nurse. I will take good care of anyone who is sick, so they never have to suffer or die.

Yours truly,
Millie

May 28
There was a lot of excitement on Drury Road today. Mama, Papa, and I were eating our lunch, when out the window we saw Mrs. Henriksson come running up the lane. Her hair was flying and her apron was flapping and she looked very upset.

Her English is not very good, so it took us a while

to understand what was wrong. But after a lot of hand waving, we figured it out: Little Anna was missing! She had been gone since morning, and all the Henrikssons were very worried.

None of us had seen her, of course, but we joined the search. "Anna! Anna!" we called. We walked through the field and the woods between our places, but we didn't find her.

When we got to the Henrikssons' place, all four boys were there (Mr. Henriksson was away and wouldn't be back until dark). Their oldest boy, Johan, told us that Anna had gone out to collect eggs from the henhouse that morning and hadn't come back.

Right at that moment, I knew where she was. I don't know how I knew. I just did.

I went to the barn and opened the door. One of the twins — I think it was Alf — said something, and although I couldn't really understand him, I knew he was saying they'd already checked the barn. I went inside, anyway.

And that's where I found her, curled up in the hay like a chickadee in a nest. She was so sound asleep that she hadn't heard them calling her name.

There was a lot of commotion then. Anna woke up and started crying. But then Mrs. Henriksson hugged me, so Anna hugged me, too. She is a pretty little girl, with blond curls and big blue eyes. She reminds me of a little china doll.

After that, we came back and finished our lunch. Mama gave me an extra slice of cake for dessert because I was a hero.

Yours truly,
Millie

May 30
Dearest friend,

I have been having the strangest dreams. Last night, I dreamed I was somewhere very bright. There were flickering lights all around me and a loud roaring noise. I kept shouting, "Get up! Get up!" I don't know why. The last time I shouted so loud, I woke myself up! It should have been funny, but the dream left me with a bad feeling. I have been grouchy all day.

Signed,
Millie the Grouch

June 1

Dearest friend,

Today I just happened to be walking by Gunner's house, and I saw him out in the lane. He was playing marbles with the Henriksson twins, Alf and Charles. Anna Henriksson was there, too, hanging around the edges because the boys wouldn't let her play.

As I have said, I don't like Gunner, so I was going to go on my way. But I couldn't leave without saying hello to Anna. I waved and shouted, "Hi, Anna!" and she waved and shouted back.

That's when I heard Gunner start talking loudly about what a swell marble collection he has, how it was "the best in the whole county." I cannot stand when Gunner starts bragging (which is all the time), so I decided to play a trick on him. I said, "Gunner, do you want to play a game?" And he said, "Fine." So I told him to hide a marble in his hand and if I guessed it right, I got to keep it, and if I guessed it wrong, I'd give him a nickel. They sell marbles three for a nickel at the general store, so Gunner thought he was getting a swell deal. Plus, he doesn't think a girl could ever beat him at anything.

So Gunner hid a marble in his hand and—surprise! I guessed it right. Gunner couldn't believe it, so we did it again, and I got it right again. Now I had two marbles! By then the twins were laughing and teasing him, and Gunner was getting steamed. We played again, only this time he put the marble in his pocket. But I guessed that right, too!

What Gunner didn't know is that I play this game with Papa all the time. Every day, Papa comes home from work with a piece of penny candy for me, and I have to try to guess which pocket it's in. I always get it right. I don't know how I know; I just do. But I'll never tell Gunner that.

Anyway, what happened next was Gunner and I got into a big fight. Gunner said I cheated and I said I didn't. And Gunner said, all matter-of-fact, "That game was gambling, and I'm going to tell your mother." I didn't like the sound of that at all, so we struck a deal. I gave Gunner two marbles back and kept one. But I kept the best one. A big green agate with a gold-and-white swirl.

I was feeling all mixed up — glad that I'd played a good trick on Gunner, but mad about giving the marbles back. I went home and got out the cigar box where I keep my special things. And then suddenly, out of nowhere, the lightbulb in my room burst with a loud POP!

I got so scared, I dropped the marble. It rolled under the bed, and disappeared. I have looked everywhere for it. But it has vanished into thin air.

CHAPTER TEN

"Casey!"

At the sound of her name, Casey looked up, startled. She turned and saw her father standing in the doorway.

"What are you doing?" he asked.

"Just reading," said Casey.

"It must be a good book. I've called you half a dozen times. Dinner will be ready soon," he told her. "Come and wash up." He disappeared back into the house.

Casey stretched. She felt stiff from sitting for so long. While she had been reading, the sun had moved across the sky, and now it made long shadows in the yard.

Setting the journal down on the swing, Casey felt in her pocket for the marble she'd found. She had been carrying it around with her ever since that first day in the house; she liked the weight of it, and sometimes she found herself absently rolling it between her fingers, like a good-luck charm.

Now Casey pulled it out and examined it more closely. The green-and-white glass swirled together, like a picture of Earth from space. Shot through it, here and there, were tiny flecks of gold.

"It's the same marble," Casey whispered. But how weird that she would find it now, after it had disappeared more than seventy years before.

"Casey!" her dad called from inside.

"Coming!" Casey called. Shoving the marble back into her pocket, she stood and went into the house.

In the kitchen, there was a large salad on the counter next to a plate of cold, sliced ham and cheese. As Casey washed her hands in the kitchen sink, her mother came in the back door. She was carrying a glass vase full of wild daisies she'd picked in the yard.

"I found the vase up in the attic. Isn't it pretty?" Mrs. Slater said. She filled it at the sink, then set it down on the kitchen table. "That really brightens up the place."

Casey agreed. The flowers gave the dreary kitchen a cheerful look.

"We're almost ready here," said Mr. Slater, who was slicing a tomato for the salad. "Casey, could you please set the table?"

Casey found forks, knives, and plates and placed them around the kitchen table. She folded some paper towels in half and placed one under each fork. Then, feeling inspired by the flowers, she got out the candles they'd used the first night and set them on the table, too.

Casey struck a match. As she leaned forward to light the first candle, she heard a loud *crack*. Suddenly, the vase shattered. Casey jumped back, dropping the match, which went out.

Her parents gasped and whirled around.

Casey stood, frozen with surprise. Water and glass covered the table. The daisies were strewn everywhere, like victims in the aftermath of a bomb.

"You cut yourself!" her mother exclaimed.

Casey looked down and saw that her hand was bleeding.

"Don't move." Her father grabbed a kitchen towel and pressed it against her hand to stop the blood. "Casey, you've got to be more careful!" he said.

"I — I didn't do anything," she stuttered. "The vase just . . . exploded."

"Let me see, now." Her father pulled away the bloodstained towel and examined the wound. "It's pretty bad, but I don't think you're going to need stitches. Just keep pressure on it for a few minutes." He wrapped her hand back up again.

"There must have been a flaw in the glass," Mrs. Slater said, wringing her hands. "I should have checked it more carefully before I put water in it. Does it hurt a lot?"

Casey shook her head, wondering how a crack in the glass could cause a vase to explode.

By the time they had cleaned up the table and bandaged Casey's hand, it was dark out. Although she had been hungry earlier, she picked at her food. Her mind was swirling with thoughts.

"Do you know anything about the people who lived here before us?" she asked her parents at last.

"People? You mean the old owners?" her father asked.

Casey nodded.

"Not much," he replied. "I heard that an old couple lived here; then it was empty for quite some time. We bought it from the bank. Why do you ask?"

"I just wondered why they would leave so much stuff behind," Casey replied. "Why didn't somebody take it?"

Her father shrugged. "It's hard to say. Maybe no one wanted it. It's possible they died without any relatives or heirs, and the bank just didn't want to go to the trouble of going through it all."

"Oh."

Casey wondered if it had been Millie who'd lived in the house, and if she had died without any relatives, with no one to give her things to. It was sad, Casey thought, that Millie would never know that her lost marble had finally been found.

That night, Casey dreamed she was looking for something in the house. She went through every room, walking at first, then starting to run. She wasn't sure what she was looking for. She only knew that it was terribly important that she find it.

By the time she reached the attic door, her heart was pounding. Slowly, she turned the doorknob. . . .

Casey awoke with a start. That was when she heard it.

Tap-tap-tap.

Tap-tap-tap-tap.

Casey pulled the sheets up to her chin. She could tell from the blackness outside her window that it was very late. Even the crickets had quit chirping. No one should have been knocking at that hour.

Tap-tap-tap.

She huddled there, barely breathing. Why didn't her parents get up? *Wake up!* she thought fiercely, hoping the silent cry would penetrate through their dreams. *Wake up!*

But they didn't stir. At last, Casey forced herself from beneath the covers. She flew down the hall, her feet barely touching the floor.

"Dad?" she said, shaking his arm. "Dad, wake up."

Her father peeled his eyes open. "What's wrong?"

"I heard someone knocking," Casey whispered.

He sat up and looked at her. "Who would be knocking this late?"

"What is it?" Casey's mother was awake now, too.

"Casey thought she heard someone knocking."

Her mother listened. "I don't hear anything."

"I heard it. Please just go look," Casey pleaded.

"All right, Casey. Calm down." Her father got out of bed and shuffled out of the room. Casey waited at the top of the stairs as he checked the front and back doors, and all the windows.

"There's no one there. Everything is locked," he said when he came back.

"I heard something," Casey insisted.

"Casey, I promise you everything is fine," her father said. "Now, why don't you go back to bed? It's very late."

"But —"

"Casey, *please*. We'll talk about it in the morning."

Casey went back to her own room. She got into bed and pulled the covers over her head. She was shaking.

Her father was wrong. Everything was *not* fine. They could lock all the doors and bolt all the windows and it still wouldn't help. Because she was sure that the knocking had come from inside the house.

CHAPTER ELEVEN

Casey awoke the next morning feeling tired and cranky. In the bright morning light, her fears from the night before seemed like a dream.

The cut on her hand was throbbing. In the bathroom, Casey checked it. It was swollen and crusted with dark blood, but it didn't look infected. She rinsed it and changed the bandages, then went down to the kitchen.

As she was eating a bowl of cereal, her mother bustled through the kitchen, carrying a bucket full of paintbrushes.

"We're painting the dining room today," she told Casey brightly. "Want to help? It'll be fun!"

Casey looked at her mother's paint-splattered T-shirt. The collar was already ringed with sweat. *There's no doubt about it,* she thought. *Mom's Fun-o-meter has gone completely haywire.* "No thanks," she said.

"How's your hand?" her mother asked.

Casey shrugged. "I'll live."

"Put a little salve on it so it doesn't get infected," her mother instructed. She frowned a little and added, "Why don't you get out of the house today? It would probably do you some good." Picking up her brushes, she left the room.

Casey finished her breakfast and rinsed her bowl in the sink. It was still early, but she could already feel sweat trickling down her back. She could tell it was going to be another scorching day.

Casey stepped onto the porch, wondering what she should do. She considered going down to the gas station to call Jillian, but the thought of riding her bike through the heat was unbearable.

Anyway, Jillian's probably busy, Casey told herself. She thought longingly of Manhattan, with its cool museums and air-conditioned movie theaters. *Lucky Jillian.*

On the porch swing, Casey spotted Millie's diary, where she'd left it the night before. She sat down and picked it up. Rocking herself gently on the swing, she opened to a random page.

June 10
Dearest friend,
I had another bad dream last night. I dreamed there was a fire. The smoke was so thick I couldn't breathe. I wanted so much to run away. But all I could do was stand there and yell, "Get up! Get up! Get up!"

That was the same dream she had before, Casey thought. She turned the page and read:

June 11
Dearest friend,
Another fire dream. This time I saw that it was our house burning. The flames climbed as high as the treetops. The heat felt like an oven. I saw the stairway collapse. But I couldn't find Mama and Papa. I looked and looked, but I couldn't find them anywhere.

These dreams always frighten me. But not as much as what happened tonight. I was lighting the candles for dinner when the candlesticks started to shake. They quivered in their holders as if they were alive. I dropped the matches and screamed for Papa. But by the time he came, they had stopped.

Despite the hot day, Casey felt a cold chill go down her spine. She turned quickly ahead, scanning the pages, until she came to this entry in the diary:

Dearest friend,

Something very strange happened today. I don't know what to make of it. I was in the kitchen, embroidering a handkerchief for my hope chest. I was in a bad mood because I hate embroidery, but Mama says I have to do it.

Mama was around the side of the house, hanging the washing on the line. Suddenly, she hollered out, "Millie, stop that!"

"Stop what?" I hollered back.

"Stop fiddling with the radio!" she yelled.

"I'm not anywhere near the radio!" I yelled back. But I went into the sitting room to see what she meant.

The radio was on so loud I had to cover my ears. But that wasn't all. It was tuning in and out <u>all by itself</u>, as if an invisible hand were turning the knobs.

I ran out of the room and yelled to Mama, but by the time she came the radio was quiet. I know Mama doesn't believe me. She thinks it is all my imagination. . . .

Casey shut the book and let it fall to the porch floor. She didn't want to read any more. Her hands were shaking and she had a funny feeling in her stomach. She felt as if she'd stumbled into one of Jaycee Woodard's spooky stories. Only this time, the main character was herself.

Casey looked across the field to the shady woods. Suddenly, she needed to get away from the house. She felt like she was suffocating there.

Casey stood and called out to her parents, "I'm going for a walk!"

"Have fun!" her mother yelled through the window.

Casey crossed the lawn quickly and set off down the road. The sun beat down on the top of her head. The droning sound of some insect filled the air like a monotonous, pulsing soundtrack.

Casey was relieved when she reached the dead-end sign and the shade of the trees. The farther Casey got from the house, the more she relaxed. She felt something loosen in her chest, like a knot unwinding.

As she walked, Casey started to notice things around her. She spotted something in the grass that looked like a golf ball, but turned out to be a mushroom that crumpled when she touched it. There were pretty blue flowers growing by the side of the road. She picked one and put it behind her ear. It made her feel a little better.

When she came to a mailbox marked GREER, Casey paused, wondering why the name sounded familiar. Then she remembered that was the tuna-casserole boy's name. Erik Greer.

Casey felt a little flutter in her stomach. She peered between the trees, and caught a glimpse of a green house with a tan car parked out front. There was no sign of life.

Across the road from Erik's house, there was

a narrower track leading between the trees. Casey could tell it wasn't a driveway, because there was no mailbox in front and she couldn't see a house nearby. She decided to follow it.

As she walked, her thoughts returned to Millie's diary. Casey couldn't deny that strange things had been happening to her ever since she had arrived at the house on Drury Road. Her parents said it was her imagination. But was it just coincidence that Millie had "imagined" the same things decades before?

The sound of running water made Casey look up. She had come to a wide woodland stream. Lost in her thoughts, she had somehow wandered off the trail.

Casey turned back to find the trail, but it wasn't there. All she saw were trees, in every direction.

Casey spun around, trying to figure out which way she'd come. *How could I be so stupid?* she thought with rising panic. *I wasn't watching where I was going, and now I'm lost! And Mom and Dad won't even think to look for me until dark. I'll be lost in the woods in the dark!*

A twig snapped somewhere nearby. Casey's stomach clenched with fear. *There are wild animals in the woods,* she thought. Why hadn't she thought of that before? There could be a mountain lion . . . or a bear! A bear that was stalking her!

Leaves rustled. Casey looked around wildly for a place to hide. But it was too late for that. She was trying to remember what you were supposed to do if you saw a bear (*Run? Stop, drop, and roll?*) when she spotted a large shape coming through the trees.

Casey covered her face and screamed. She heard a crash of leaves, followed by a low curse. Something about the voice was familiar. . . .

"Erik?" Casey said, peeking through her hands.

She followed the thrashing noises and found him lying on his back, tangled up in a bush. He frowned up at her. "Why do you scream every time you see me? Am I really that scary?"

"I thought you were a bear," Casey admitted. She glanced around just to be sure that a bear hadn't been following Erik. "I'm scared of bears."

"Well, nothing to worry about now. If there were any bears nearby, you've probably scared them all to death." When Casey didn't reply, he added, "Are you going to help me up or what?"

Casey grasped his hand and pulled him out of the bush. There were leaves stuck to his shirt, and his bare arms were covered with little red scratches. "What are you doing here?" she asked.

"I always come down here when it's hot. The stream is the only place to cool off," Erik said, brushing at the leaves on his shirt.

"There's one in your hair," Casey said, pulling it out.

"Thanks. So, what are *you* doing here?" he asked.

Casey suddenly remembered her problem. "I'm lost!" she told him. "Thank goodness you showed up. Do you have any idea how to get back to the trail?"

Erik stared at her. Then a smile crept across his face. "It's about ten feet that way. You can't miss it," he said, pointing in the direction he had come.

Casey could tell he was laughing at her again. She straightened her shoulders. "Thank you," she said coldly with as much dignity as she could muster. "Have fun at your stream." She started toward the trail.

"Wait," Erik said, chasing after her. "You can't go yet."

Casey stopped. "Why not?"

"You'll, uh . . . miss the regatta!"

"The what?"

"The regatta. You know, like a boat race," Erik said.

Casey looked back at the stream, confused. It didn't seem deep enough for any kind of boat.

Erik was bent over, searching for something on the ground. "Find a stick," he told her.

She didn't have a clue what he was up to, but she picked up a long stick. "You mean, like this?"

"Ah," Erik said, nodding. "A classic schooner. Me, I tend to prefer a skiff." He held up a much smaller twig. "We're going to race them," he told Casey. "That log is the starting point. We'll go all the way to the bend in the stream. Ready?"

"I guess," Casey said. It seemed a little silly to her. *But why not?* she thought. It wasn't like she had anything better to do.

They took their sticks over to the half-submerged log. "On your mark," said Erik. "Get set. . . . Go!"

They both dropped the sticks into the water. At once, the current carried them away. Erik ran alongside the stream, shouting encouragement to his stick. Casey ran after him, laughing and shouting, too.

"Come on, come on! To the right! Watch out for that log!" Erik yelled.

"Go, go, go, go . . . no, no!" Casey hollered as her stick headed toward a tangle of roots.

As she nudged it free, Erik's stick got caught on a rock. He threw pebbles at it to knock it loose.

"Ha-ha!" Casey shouted. "I'm winning!"

"The race isn't over yet!" Erik warned as his boat sped after hers.

In the end, Erik won by a small margin, but Casey was laughing too much to care. "So is this what people do for fun in Stillness?" she asked him.

Erik shrugged. "Not everyone. I guess it probably seems boring to you. What do you do for fun . . . wherever it is you're from?"

"New York," Casey replied. "I hang out with my friends. My best friend, Jillian, mostly. We go shopping and listen to music, that kind of stuff. We had all these great plans for this summer, before I found out I was coming here." Casey wasn't sure why she was telling Erik this, but it felt good to talk to someone.

"What kind of plans?" he asked.

"Like going to Six Flags and to the beach." Casey decided to leave out the part about finding boyfriends. "Anyway, Jillian's been doing all that stuff without me. So at least one of us is having a good summer." She sighed.

"Beach," Erik said with a dismissive wave. "Who needs the beach when you can have your own private island?"

"What do you mean?" Casey asked.

He smiled. "Follow me."

Erik led the way around a little bend in the stream. "There," he said, pointing.

A large, mossy boulder jutted up like an island in the middle of the stream. Part of its top had broken away, forming a sort of bench. It looked like a perfect place to sit. "See? My own private island," said Erik.

"Cool! But how do you get out there?" Casey

asked. The stream was at least two feet deep and flowing fast.

Erik went to the water's edge and stepped out onto a dry rock poking up from the surface. With light hops, he skipped from rock to rock in the stream, until he had reached the boulder. He looked back at Casey. "Come on."

Casey hesitantly stepped onto the first rock. Holding her arms out for balance, she took another small step forward.

"Now there," said Erik, pointing to a bit of dry rock peeking up from the water.

Casey reached for it. It wobbled beneath her foot, and she gasped.

"It's okay," said Erik. "Just go fast."

The next rock was wide, but it was far away and it looked slippery. Casey glanced down at the water rushing around her feet. "I can't do it."

"Yes you can," said Erik. "Two more steps, and you're there."

Casey tried to step forward, but her legs seemed to be frozen. She hovered there for a long moment. "I'm scared," she said finally.

Erik leaned forward and held out his hand. It was just out of Casey's reach. "Come on," he said. "What's the worst thing that can happen?"

Casey thought about that. "I'll get wet."

"Exactly," he said.

Casey took a deep breath. Mustering all her courage, she leaped onto the slippery rock. Her foot started to slide. But a second later, Erik's hand was grasping hers and he was pulling her onto the island.

"Not too bad for a city girl," he said.

Casey made a face.

They settled onto the mossy bench, leaning their backs against the cool stone. Sunlight filtered through the leaves of the trees overhead, dappling their legs.

For a while they just sat listening to the water. Casey was surprised at how nice it felt. Boys usually made her nervous.

Eventually, Erik turned to her and asked, "What happened to your hand?"

Casey looked down at the bandage. Instead of answering, she said, "What do you know about our house?"

"What do you mean?"

"There's something weird about it, isn't there?"

Erik didn't answer at first. He picked up a twig and began to peel off the bark. He looked like he was considering what to say. "Some folks think that place is haunted," he told her finally.

A shiver went down Casey's spine. She'd had the exact same thought, but it was scarier to hear someone say it out loud. "What have you heard?" she asked, not sure she wanted to know the answer.

"Spooky stories. Weird noises. Voices calling for help. I heard about some kids who broke in one time. Maybe they were hoping they could steal some stuff, or maybe it was a dare. All I know is, they got real scared. They didn't last twenty minutes in there."

And I'm living *there,* Casey thought with a shudder. "How come you didn't want to tell me?"

"I guess I didn't want to scare you." Erik glanced sideways at her. "You are kinda jumpy."

"I am not!" Casey exclaimed. "Okay. Well, maybe just a little," she admitted when he gave her a look.

"Anyway, I don't really believe all those stories," he told her. "My gran always said it was a lot of claptrap. She'd get real mad about it, too. If my friends or me ever started telling stories about that place, she'd tell us to hush up. And she ought to know. She's lived around here her whole life."

Casey remembered how Erik had backed away when her mother had invited him in. "So if you don't believe any of it, how come you wouldn't come inside?" she teased.

Erik looked at Casey curiously. "What about you? Do *you* believe it?"

Casey hesitated. He'd laughed at her before. What if he laughed at her now? At the same time, she felt desperate to talk to someone.

"I get a weird feeling," she admitted. "Like . . . like something is there, some presence. Then the other night, out of nowhere, this vase shattered. That's how I cut my hand." She fiddled with the bandage. "And last night I heard someone knocking. Weird, huh?"

She glanced quickly at Erik and was relieved to see that he wasn't smiling.

"What do your parents say?" he asked.

"They don't say anything. Half the time, they don't even notice. They think I'm imagining things."

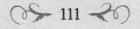

"That's tough." Erik threw the twig into the water and watched it float away downstream. "If there is a ghost, what kind of ghost do you think it is?" he wondered.

What kind of question was that? "A scary one, obviously," Casey said.

"I mean, is it a lost soul?" Erik mused. "Or a wandering spirit . . . or a demon from hell? Just kidding," he added quickly when Casey turned pale. "It's probably not a demon from hell."

"I sure hope not!"

"Anyway, there are lots of kinds of ghosts. Did you know that some people think poltergeists might actually be a form of psychic activity?" Erik turned to Casey, his eyes bright with sudden interest. "Do you think you might be psychic?"

"I — I don't know," Casey stuttered, surprised at this conversation twist.

Erik tucked a hand behind his back. "How many fingers am I holding up?"

"Three," Casey guessed.

"Nope. One. What's my favorite color?"

Casey squinted thoughtfully. "Blue?"

"Orange. What's my mother's maiden name?"

"Er . . . Smith?"

Erik shook his head. "You are definitely not psychic."

"I never said I was," Casey retorted. *What a strange guy Erik is turning out to be,* she thought. *Strange, but interesting.* "How do you know all this stuff about ghosts and psychics, anyway?"

"TV." Erik shrugged as if it were obvious. "Don't you watch cable?"

"Not *those* kinds of shows," said Casey. "Too scary."

"Cable TV. Wild animals. Crossing streams. Boys named Erik." He ticked them off on his fingers. "Is there anything that *doesn't* scare you?"

"No," said Casey. Then she added, "Well, maybe not boys named Erik."

Erik grinned. Then he leaned back against the rock, with one hand behind his head. "Anyway, it's too bad you don't know what kind of ghost it is," he said. "At least then you'd know what you were dealing with."

They sat there awhile longer. When the sun moved directly overhead, Erik stood up. "I'd better get going. I told my mom I'd be home for lunch."

Casey reluctantly got up, too. She wasn't looking forward to going back to the house.

"You first this time," Erik said as they began to make their way back across.

Gingerly, Casey stepped out onto the rocks. She was halfway across when Erik suddenly gave her a push from behind. She lost her balance and splashed into the stream, falling in up to her knees.

"What did you do that for?!" Casey shrieked.

"Not so bad, right?" Erik said.

Cold water rushed around Casey's legs. After she'd recovered from the shock of falling, she realized it felt surprisingly good.

Erik grinned. "Now you have one less thing to be afraid of."

CHAPTER TWELVE

Casey squelched home in wet sneakers. As she walked through the front door, she was hit with the smell of paint.

"Hello! Anyone home?" Casey poked her head into the living room. It looked bright with fresh white paint, except for one wall that had been painted brickred. The paint still looked wet, and there were brushes and rollers strewn around, but the room was empty. Somewhere in another part of the house, she could hear someone hammering.

Casey sighed and climbed the stairs. In her bedroom she took off her wet shoes and socks, laying them on the windowsill to dry, then changed out of her sweaty T-shirt.

As Casey was pulling a clean tank top over her head, she suddenly became aware of a different sound. It was softer than the hammering, but just as steady.

Tap-tap-tap-tap.

Casey paused and listened. There was a long pause; then it came again. Beneath it, Casey thought she heard the faint sound of someone crying.

She went out into the hallway. "Mom?" she called. "Dad?"

There was no answer. The hammering had stopped. Casey listened again. The muffled noise was louder now. *It definitely sounds like crying,* she thought.

She followed the sound to the end of the hall. At the door to the attic, she stopped. The crying seemed to be coming from somewhere overhead.

Casey hesitated with her hand on the knob. She'd avoided the attic ever since the day she'd gone up there with her mother.

But what if Mom or Dad is up there? she thought. *Maybe they went up to the attic and something fell on them. They could be hurt!*

Taking a deep breath, she turned the knob. In the narrow stairwell, the sound of crying was clear. Casey was sure she heard someone call, "Help me!"

"I'm coming!" Casey yelled, her feet pounding the steps. She had a terrible vision of one of her parents lying injured above her.

The tapping was back, and louder now. The sound swelled into thumps, then bangs. Someone was pounding violently against something, as if trying to get out.

"I'm coming!" Casey shrieked again.

She emerged into the attic, practically stumbling into the room. Casey looked around frantically. The room was empty.

But she could still hear the desperate pounding. It was coming from the corner of the attic.

Casey started toward the sound, but halfway there she froze. Her blood turned to ice. The thumps were coming from inside the steamer trunk.

Casey didn't remember turning and leaving the room. The next thing she knew, she was scrambling down the staircase, screaming for her parents.

She heard footsteps, and suddenly her parents were in the hallway, their eyes wide with surprise and concern. Casey threw herself into her mother's arms.

"There's something up there!" she cried. "There's something in the attic!"

"Casey, what is it?" her mother exclaimed. "What happened?"

"Someone was knocking and crying!" Casey was crying herself now. "They were calling for help!"

"A *person*?" Her father looked alarmed. He brushed past her, headed for the stairs.

"Don't go up there!" Casey screamed. But her dad was already taking the steps two at a time.

"Joe, be careful!" her mother called worriedly.

"It's the ghost, Mom! It's the ghost. I know it is!" Casey clung to her mother like a baby. Her mother held her and didn't say anything.

A moment later, Casey's father came back down the stairs.

"There's nothing up there," he said. He and Casey's mother exchanged a look.

"But I *heard* something!" Casey said.

"It could have been an animal," her father told

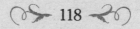

her. "The window was open. A raccoon or some other critter could have crawled in. Whatever it was, it's gone now."

"It wasn't an *animal*! I heard a voice. A human voice. It was saying, 'Help me!' It was coming from the steamer trunk!"

"The steamer trunk was wide open," her father reported. "And it was empty."

This news went through Casey like an electric shock. "It was closed before. I know it was."

"It was locked the other day," Casey's mother said, her brow furrowing. "I couldn't find the key."

"Well, someone must have found it." Casey's father looked at Casey meaningfully.

"It wasn't me." She took a step back.

He thinks I'm playing some kind of joke, she realized suddenly. *He thinks I'm making it all up.* "It wasn't me," she repeated. "Don't you understand? This house is haunted! We have to get out of here!"

"Calm down, Casey. . . ." her father began.

"I won't calm down!" she screeched, her voice rising to a hysterical pitch. Tears began streaming down her cheeks again. "Why won't you believe me? *There is something terrible in this house!*"

"Casey, *that's enough*!" her father shouted.

Casey was so surprised she stopped crying. Her father had never yelled at her like that before.

He took a deep breath, running his hands through his hair. "Now, I understand you don't like it here." His voice was low with barely controlled anger. "But this behavior has got to stop. Your mother and I have put a lot into this house. This is our dream, and you are just going to have to make it work. All this sulking and stomping around. The nighttime antics, and this ridiculous talk about ghosts — I'm sick of it. Do you hear me, Casey? *It has got to stop.*"

Casey stared at him, stunned. She looked over at her mother. Mrs. Slater was silent, but Casey could tell from the look on her face that she agreed with Casey's dad.

Without another word, Casey spun on her heel and ran to her room.

She flung herself down on her bed, weeping. The house was haunted; she was sure of that now. Casey was more frightened than she'd ever been. She felt certain that they were in danger, but for the first time in her life, she couldn't count on her parents to protect her. And if they didn't believe her, there was nothing she could do.

"I'm trapped," Casey sobbed into her pillow. "Trapped."

Over the next few days, things got worse. Casey mostly avoided her parents during the day, preferring to go for walks or stay in her room reading. Dinner was a mostly silent affair, punctuated by scrupulous politeness. ("Could you please pass the salt? Thank you." "Would you like some more peas?" "No thank you." "How is your steak?" "Fine, thank you.") The tension that had simmered in the house all summer had risen to a boil.

As if in response to the uneasy atmosphere, the ghostly activity increased. Dishes rattled, windows slammed shut, books tumbled from shelves. Once, Casey tripped over a toolbox that had suddenly moved from one place to another and bruised her toe badly. She never mentioned any of these incidents to her parents. What would be the point?

But a cold knot of fear lodged in her chest, like an ice cube that had gotten stuck going halfway down.

Twice Casey went back to the stream, hoping to run into Erik, but he was never there. Once, she started up his driveway, thinking she might find him at home. But halfway to the house, she saw a face gazing at her from a window. Casey gave a tentative wave. But the figure in the window just stared at her blankly, and Casey got intimidated and ran away.

"What could Erik do, anyway?" Casey told herself gruffly, trying to brush away her disappointment. "He's just a kid like me."

In the end, Casey spent most of her time with Millie. She had started reading the diary again. In it, she found a friend whose experiences almost mirrored her own.

June 29,

Dearest friend,

Today Mama and Papa were out, and I was reading in my room, when I heard the front door slam. I thought that they were back, so I went down to say hello. But nobody was there. I ran back up to my room and hid there until they got home.

July 5
Dearest friend,

Canning day today. Mama had two bushels of berries, and she was bound and determined to can every single one. Of course, she gave me the task of boiling all the jars.

It was horribly hot in the kitchen, and the longer we were in there, the worse I started to feel. Not just because of the heat, but because I could tell something bad was going to happen.

And then it did. When Mama's back was turned, three of the jars burst right in a row — POP, POP, POP! It sounded like guns going off, and there was juice splatter and glass splinters everywhere. Mama thought I had broken them somehow, but I hadn't! Why do these things keep happening? I have heard that there are devils and spirits who choose one person to torment. Is it a devil following me?

As she read, Casey searched the pages for clues for who or what the ghost might be. But Millie didn't seem to know either. As the diary went on, she wrote less and less about her experiences, and more about her dreams.

August 2
Dearest friend,
Every night I live through another fire. Smoke and ashes fill my dreams. It's gotten so I hardly want to close my eyes. The sight of a candle flame starts me trembling. . . .

August 8
Dear friend,
Today when I was in my room, I happened to glance in the mirror over the dressing table. I saw my face — and yet, it wasn't my face. I saw my round cheeks and my dark eyes, but my face was smudged with soot and ash. My hair was a tangled black cloud, and smoke billowed all around me. I saw myself caught in the fire!

I screamed for Mama, but when I told her about it, she said it was just my imagination running wild. She said I have been reading too many silly books. She took all my adventure novels then and put them away somewhere. But I don't think this was from too much reading. I have never read a story like this. . . .

August 12
Friend,
Mama and Papa are worried. They think I am growing too thin. "You need to eat," they say when I pick at my food. But I have no appetite. How can I eat when I have a feeling that something terrible is going to happen?

August 14
F,
I have started to have a new dream. There is no smoke or flames, but somehow it is even more terrible than my fire dreams. In this dream, it is very dark and I am all alone. I think Mama and Papa must be looking for me. I call their names again and again. But they never hear me and they never come. . . .

At night, Casey dreamed, too. But her dreams were never about fire. Over and over, she dreamed she was playing hide-and-seek in the house.

Sometimes she was hiding; other times she was the one searching. These dreams had a sense of urgency, and always, just before she awoke, Casey heard a singsong voice cry out, *"Ready or not, here I come. . . ."*

CHAPTER THIRTEEN

One week after the steamer trunk incident, Casey came to the end of Millie's journal. It was dated *August 22*, and as usual, it began, *Dearest friend.*

> *I am going to have a party today! Mama and Papa are throwing it, and they won't even tell me why. It isn't my birthday or anything. Papa said, "Who needs a reason for a party?" They have planned all kinds of games and things. "Now, if that doesn't put a smile back on your face, I don't know what will," Papa told me.*
>
> *We have invited children from all over Stillness —sixteen altogether. Edie Finney is coming from way out on North Road. Also, Grace Evanston, Pearl Miller,*

the Avery girls and baby Jackie, Nathan and Rose Hopkins, George Archer, Gretchen Forsyth, and of course the Henrikssons — Johan, Peter, the twins, Alf and Charles, and little Anna. I have even invited Gunner Anderson, although he does not really deserve it.

Mama has been working on the cake all morning. It has yellow icing and sugar roses. I am going to wear my best dress, and as soon as Mama is done with the cake she is going to braid ribbons into my hair.

The only bad thing is that there were clouds when I woke up this morning. I hope they go away. I don't want a single drop of rain to spoil my perfect party.

I am so excited. I think I may burst waiting for it to begin!

Yours truly,
Millie

Casey turned to the next page, but it was blank. So was the next. She flipped to the end of the journal, then went back again and checked each page carefully. There wasn't so much as a single word.

Casey closed the diary, feeling troubled. She couldn't imagine why Millie would stop writing.

Maybe she made a new friend at the party, Casey told herself, *so she had someone to talk to and didn't need her diary anymore.*

But that didn't seem right. After all, Millie wrote about everything in her diary. Wouldn't she write about making a new friend, too?

"It doesn't really matter," Casey told herself. "It all happened a long time ago."

She set the journal aside and went downstairs. Her parents had finished painting the living room and were now working on the second room, running rollers of white paint up and down the walls. Casey skirted the paint-splattered drop cloths and went out to the porch. On the swing, she put on her head-phones and tried to listen to No Tomorrow. But for once the moody music didn't soothe her. She couldn't shake the thought of Millie from her mind.

Finally, she took off her headphones and got her bike.

"I'm going for a ride," she called through the dining room window to her mother.

"Be back before dinner!" her mother called back.

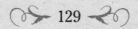

Casey pedaled to the gas station and called Jillian. To her relief, her friend picked up on the second ring.

"Casey!" Jillian shrieked. "You called at totally the best time! I'm about to meet up with David to go to this concert in Central Park. Do you think I should wear my zebra-striped mini or that orange sundress I got at the Salvation Army?"

"I don't know," said Casey. "Jillian, listen, I need to talk to you. I'm really worried about something."

"Case, what's wrong?" Jillian asked, her voice suddenly filled with concern.

"It's complicated," Casey said. She launched into the story of finding Millie's diary in the attic, Millie's eerie predictions and her disturbing dreams, and the abrupt way the diary ended.

"She was going to a party and she was really excited," Casey explained. "I can't understand why she'd suddenly just stop writing. I'm worried, Jillian. I have this feeling something bad happened —"

"Hold on," Jillian interrupted. "You're not making sense. You said you found this diary in the attic and it's really old, right?"

"Uh-huh. It was written in 1939."

"So . . . I don't get it. What are you so worried about? I mean, for all you know, she could be *dead*."

Casey gulped. "That's what I'm afraid of," she whispered.

There was silence on the other end of the line. Then Jillian cleared her throat. "Look, Casey, I don't know how to say this, but you're acting really weird. Why are you freaking out about someone who lived, like, forever ago?"

Casey paused, searching for the words. How could she explain to Jillian that Millie felt as real to her as Jillian — as real as Casey herself? That what happened to Millie *did* matter. It mattered a lot.

On the other end of the line, Casey heard the buzzer to Jillian's apartment.

"Oh, sugar," Jillian said. "That's David, and I haven't even finished getting dressed. I have to go. Are you going to be okay?"

"Sure," Casey said, trying to make her voice light. "I'm fine."

"Call me later. Promise?" said Jillian.

"Okay."

Casey hung up the phone, feeling rattled and confused. Jillian was right, of course. If Millie wasn't dead by now, she was at least very, very old. But it was hard for Casey to imagine her that way. To her, Millie would always be the girl she was in her diary.

Jillian was too busy to listen, and Casey knew that her parents wouldn't understand. But there was still one person who might.

Casey wheeled her bike up the driveway to Erik's house. She could see toys scattered around the yard. Two little kids were playing in front of the house. They both had short curly blond hair like Erik's.

"Hi there," Casey said as she drew up close. "I'm looking for Erik. Is he around?"

Two kids gaped at her like she'd flown up in a spaceship. Then one of them leaped up and ran around the side of the house. The other remained, warily watching Casey as if she might try to make off with a tricycle or something.

A moment later, Erik came around the side of the house. Casey felt her heart do a little jump.

"Hey!" he said when he saw Casey. He sounded surprised. "What's up?"

"I was just riding by. I thought you might be home," Casey told him. For a second she wasn't sure what to say. She glanced down at the little kid, who was still regarding her suspiciously. "Are these your, uh . . ." Casey trailed off, unsure if they were boys or girls.

"Sisters," Erik filled in quickly. "This is Bridget and that's Bee, short for Beatrice. Don't worry if you can't tell them apart. Almost no one can. They're identical."

The twin closest to him tugged his hand, and when he leaned down, she whispered in his ear. Erik glanced at Casey and laughed.

"What?" asked Casey.

"She says you're pretty," Erik told her. He smiled and added, "She wants to know if you're my girlfriend."

Casey blushed, and Erik laughed again. "You want to come in?" he asked.

"Sure," Casey said.

"You, too," Erik told the twins. "You can't be outside alone."

Erik led the way into the house. In the living room, there were children's toys strewn everywhere, and Casey heard the TV going in another room. The whole place was messy in a comfortable way. Casey liked it much better than her own house.

Erik shooed the twins into the room with the TV. "Come meet my mom," he said to Casey.

Casey followed him into the kitchen. A woman was sitting at the table, surrounded by pieces of paper. She had blond hair pulled back in a bun and pale gray eyes like Erik's.

"Mom, this is Casey Slater," Erik said. "She just moved into the house at the end of the lane."

"Nice to meet you," Casey said politely. "Thank you for the casserole."

The woman gave her a tired smile. "I'm glad you liked it. It's as easy to make two as it is to make one."

"It was delicious," Casey fibbed.

Erik's mother nodded. "Nice to meet you, Casey," she said, and turned back to her papers.

Erik got two cans of soda from the refrigerator and led the way into the living room. He cleared some stuffed animals off the couch, and they sat down.

"Mom's a little distracted. She's always like that

on bill day," Erik said. He popped open his soda can. "So what's up?"

"I didn't come over just because I was riding by," Casey confessed. "I wanted to talk to you. There've been more weird things happening. At my house."

Erik's expression grew serious. He waited for Casey to go on.

She told him about the past week — the crying in the attic, the doors slamming, and things falling. Then she told him about Millie's journal. It took a long time to explain, and sometimes the things she said sounded crazy, even to her own ears. But Erik listened without interrupting, a little frown of concentration on his face.

"For a while I thought maybe my parents were right. Maybe it was all in my head," Casey told him. "But I don't think that's true anymore. Things have been happening to me just the same as they did to Millie. And then when I came to the end of her diary . . . " She trailed off, unable to finish the thought.

Erik finished it for her. "You're afraid that whatever happened to Millie could happen to you, too."

Casey nodded, relieved that Erik didn't think she was nuts.

"But you don't know that anything happened to her," Erik pointed out. "She could have just lost her diary or moved or something."

"I know," Casey admitted. "But . . . I just have a feeling something bad happened."

From another room, a shrill voice suddenly called out, "Charles!" Casey jumped, startled.

"That's my gran," said Erik, getting to his feet. "I'd better go see what she wants. You can come, if you want."

Casey got up and followed Erik to the TV room. She was surprised to see an old woman sitting in a chair by the window. Casey hadn't noticed her before. The woman had a pale face and a down-turned mouth, and at once Casey recognized her as the face she'd seen in the window that day. The woman's lap was covered with a blue crocheted blanket. She stared vacantly at the TV, where the twins were watching cartoons.

"She might seem a little confused," Erik warned Casey. "Gran's memory's not so good anymore." He went over to the old woman and gently touched her shoulder. She looked up, startled.

"Hey, Gran. It's me," he said.

She blinked at him. "Charles?"

"No, Erik. Your grandson," he said patiently. "I have someone I want you to meet. This is my friend Casey."

Gran's gaze slid past Erik. When she saw Casey, her expression brightened. "You're back!" she exclaimed.

"I'm sorry," Casey told her. "You must be mistaken. I've never been here be —"

"You're back!" Gran insisted, her voice girlish and lilting. She looked into Casey's face, her eyes shining. "I've missed you so much, Millie."

CHAPTER FOURTEEN

Casey stared at the old woman in horror. "Why did you call me *Millie*?"

"No, Gran," Erik said. "Her name is Casey. My friend *Casey*."

Gran didn't seem to hear him. She reached out and grasped Casey's hand in her bony one. "I'm so happy to see you, Millie. I looked for you everywhere. We all looked for you."

Casey felt the urge to wrench her hand away, but she resisted it. Erik's grandmother knew something about Millie, and this might be Casey's only chance to find out.

"What do you know?" she asked urgently. "Do you know what happened to Millie?"

The old woman stared at her. Then she dropped Casey's hand. "It's not my fault," she said.

"What do you mean? What's not your fault?" Casey pressed.

Gran looked back and forth between Erik and Casey. In a second, her eyes clouded with anger. "Who are you?" she asked, her voice suddenly harsh. "Charles, who is this? What is she doing in my house?"

She was almost shouting. The twins turned from the TV to stare.

"I'm Casey," Casey told her. "Erik's friend Casey. I need to know what happened to Millie."

"Get out of my house!"

"It's no use." Erik put a hand on Casey's arm and pulled her away. "She can't remember anything."

Gran's lips worked soundlessly. She was trembling, but whether from anger or fear Casey wasn't sure. Erik poured his grandmother a glass of water from a pitcher on a side table. Then he and Casey quietly left the room.

"I'm sorry," Casey said when they were out in the hall. "I didn't mean to upset her."

"It's okay," Erik said. "She gets confused really

easily. She calls me Charles — that was one of her brothers' names. The twins, too. Sometimes she even forgets who my mom is."

"But she knew Millie," Casey said. "She acted like they were old friends."

"It sure seemed that way," Erik agreed.

The wheels in Casey's mind were turning. Something Erik said had sounded familiar. "Your grandmother had brothers?"

"Four of them," Erik replied. "Why?"

"What were their names?" Casey asked, though she had a feeling she already knew the answer.

"Well, one was Charles, of course. And the others were Peter, Alfred, and John — Johan, that is."

Casey nodded slowly. "And your grandmother's name is Anna. Anna Henriksson."

Erik's mouth fell open. "How did you know that?"

"Millie's diary," Casey told him. "She wrote about the Henrikssons. They were her closest neighbors." She could picture their names in Millie's handwriting, just as clearly as if the diary were in front of her.

Erik exhaled with relief. "For a second there, I thought you really were psychic."

"But do you see what this means?" Casey said. "Your grandmother and her brothers knew Millie, which means they may know what happened to her!"

"There's just one problem," Erik said. "Gran doesn't remember anything. And all her brothers are dead."

Casey chewed her lip thoughtfully. "Then there must be someone else," she said at last. "There were a lot of children at that party. There must be someone alive who can still remember it."

It had gotten darker in the living room, and Erik switched a lamp on.

"Jeez!" cried Casey, leaping up from the couch. "I didn't realize how late it was. I'd better get home or my mom will freak."

Erik walked Casey to the door. "Tomorrow we'll go through the journal and look for clues," he promised. He glanced out at the dusk. A stiff wind had come up and was bending the tops of the trees. "Are you going to be okay riding home?"

"I'll be fine," Casey said. "See you tomorrow."

Outside, she was surprised at how much the temperature had dropped. It had been warm when she left her house, but she was suddenly freezing in her shorts and T-shirt. She battled a headwind all the way back, and was chilled to the bone by the time she got home.

Her mother was in the kitchen when Casey came through the back door. "I was starting to get worried about you," she said. "Where have you been?"

"I ran into Erik," Casey told her. "You know, the boy with the tuna casserole." She rubbed her bare arms. "Why is it so cold?"

"There must be a storm coming in," her mother replied. "Your dad's got a fire going in the living room. Why don't you run in there and warm up? Dinner should be ready soon."

Casey hurried into the living room. Her dad was standing there with his hands on his hips, looking proudly at the fire blazing in the fireplace.

"I had a heck of a time getting it started," he told Casey. "Smoke kept pouring into the room, even though the flue was open. Whatever the problem was, it's fixed itself now. Come get warmed up. I'm going to go help Mom with dinner."

Casey stretched out gratefully on the rug in front of the fireplace. She wanted to think more about

Erik's gran. *What had she meant when she said, "It's not my fault"?* Casey wondered.

But after the excitement of the day and her cold ride home, Casey was deeply tired. The smell of food cooking soothed her, and the heat from the fire made her sleepy. Before she knew it, her eyes had closed.

Casey couldn't have said how long she was asleep. She woke to a jarring crash.

Casey sat up with a gasp. The room seemed to be in shambles. Books and broken glass were everywhere. It took Casey a moment to put together what had happened. A heavy old china cabinet where Casey's parents had been storing their tools and home improvement books had toppled over, landing just inches from where Casey was lying.

Her parents came rushing into the room. "Casey, what happened?" her father exclaimed.

Casey knew what had happened. But she also knew her parents wouldn't believe her. "I don't know. The cabinet fell," she told them.

"There's no way that cabinet could have just fallen over," her father said. "It's got to weigh more than a hundred pounds." He looked at Casey, still sitting on the rug, and she could see him calculating that she was not strong enough to move it herself. For the first time she saw a flicker of doubt and confusion in his eyes.

Her mother looked shaken as she helped Casey up. "It's not safe," she murmured. "You could have been killed."

An unused can of paint had been crushed beneath the cabinet, and now a crimson puddle seeped across the floor. Casey stared at it in horror. *That could have been me,* she thought. Now more than ever she knew she needed to find out what happened to Millie. Her own life depended on it!

CHAPTER FIFTEEN

That night, the wind blew in a storm. Rain lashed against Casey's window, and outside the trees rustled and swayed. Every rattling windowpane or creak of the house sounded like the ghost coming for her.

The storm finally died out sometime around dawn. When the sun started to rise, Casey got out of bed, feeling tired and shaky. She pulled on a pair of jeans and a sweatshirt, not bothering to comb her hair. She wrote her parents a note and left it on the kitchen table. Then she slipped out the back door.

Wispy clouds, red with dawn, trailed across the sky. The storm had broken the heat wave, and the air felt cool and clean.

Casey had been worried that she would have to wait around outside Erik's house until someone woke up. So she was surprised to see him waiting for her on the front steps.

"You don't look so great," Erik greeted her.

Casey gave him a half smile. "Good morning to you, too." She sat down next to him on the steps, and pulled Millie's diary out of the front pocket of her sweatshirt.

"So what exactly are we looking for?" Erik asked.

"I thought we should start with the names of the kids from Millie's party. Maybe you'll recognize one of them," Casey said. "If we can find them, they might be able to tell us something."

She turned to Millie's last entry, and began to read the list of names. " 'Edie Finney, Grace Evanston, Pearl Miller, the Avery girls —' "

"There's a Mrs. Avery at my school," Erik interrupted. "She teaches eighth grade English."

"Is she old?" asked Casey.

"Pretty old," Erik said. "At least forty."

Casey rolled her eyes. "Erik, if she's forty, she wouldn't even have been born yet in 1939. We're looking for someone your gran's age, at least."

"Oh," said Erik. "Right."

Casey went back to her list. "'Baby Jackie' — I guess he was an Avery, too — Nathan and Rose Hopkins, George Archer, Gretchen Forsyth, and the Henrikssons — Johan, Peter, Alf, Charles, and Anna.' Oh, and then there's this boy, Gunner Anderson. He was in her diary a lot."

"Anderson," Erik murmured. He had plucked a long piece of grass and was chewing the end thoughtfully. "There's a Mr. Anderson who lives closer in toward town."

"Is he old?"

Erik nodded. "Stingy, too. I mowed his lawn for him once. It took all afternoon, and he only paid me two dollars."

Casey closed the diary and stood up. "Let's try him. At least it's a start."

Mr. Anderson lived in a small white house, close to the end of Main Street. Casey and Erik left their bikes at the edge of the yard, and started up his walkway.

"I guess word got around that he doesn't

pay for yard work," Erik said, eyeing the over-grown lawn.

At the door, Casey reached for the doorbell, then hesitated. "Do you think it's too early?" she asked Erik. It wasn't even seven thirty yet.

"Doubt it," said Erik. "If he's anything like Gran, he was up at the crack of dawn."

Casey took a deep breath and rang the bell.

They heard shuffling inside. After what seemed like an eternity, the door opened a crack. A man's face peeked out around the door chain. "Yes? What is it?" he asked gruffly.

Casey stared. It was the man from the grocery store. The one who had seemed so frightened of her.

Erik stepped forward. "Hi, Mr. Anderson. You remember me? Erik Greer? I mowed your lawn once."

Mr. Anderson didn't reply. His gaze slid past Erik to Casey, and in his eyes Casey saw a flicker of fear. *Why does he seem so afraid of me?* she wondered.

"This is my friend Casey," Erik continued. "Casey Slater. She just moved to town."

Casey gave Mr. Anderson what she hoped was a

friendly, reassuring smile. "We were hoping we could talk to you."

"About what?" he asked.

"Millie Hughes. She used to live in the house at the end of Drury Road. We wondered if you knew her."

There was a pause; then the door closed in their faces.

Is that it? Casey thought, her heart sinking. But a second later, she heard the scrape of the chain being undone. The door opened wide, revealing Mr. Anderson. He was dressed in pressed pants, a button-down sweater, and a pair of worn brown slippers.

"Your name's Casey, is it?" he asked her.

She nodded.

Mr. Anderson gave her a long look. "Well, Casey," he said at last. "Why don't you and Erik come in and tell me why you want to know about Millie."

Despite its neglected lawn, the inside of Mr. Anderson's house was neat and tidy. Casey and Erik sat on the couch, while Mr. Anderson poured them cups of tea from a chipped teapot.

"So you knew Millie?" Casey asked, sipping the hot liquid.

"Yes, I did." Mr. Anderson sat back in an easy chair. "We lived near each other on Drury Road a long, long time ago. How do you know about Millie, may I ask?"

"I found her diary. And I read . . . some of it," Casey fibbed. She wondered if he would think it was wrong. "She mentioned you."

Mr. Anderson raised his eyebrows. "Did she? What did she say?"

"Well . . ." Casey glanced at Erik. ". . . she said you thought too highly of yourself. But I think she liked you," she added quickly.

The old man chuckled, but it sounded sad. "She was right. I *did* think too highly of myself. Millie was quite a girl," he told them. "Sharp as a whip. You couldn't get a thing past her."

"Can you tell us what happened to her?" Erik asked.

Mr. Anderson was silent. Finally, he said, "Are you sure you want to know? It's not a very nice story."

"We want to know," Erik said. Casey nodded.

"There was a party at Millie's," Mr. Anderson said. "Just about all the children we knew were invited. It was going to be the event of the summer."

"Millie wrote about it in her diary," Casey told him. "She was really excited. She couldn't wait for it to start."

Mr. Anderson nodded. "Everyone was excited. After the cake, there were lots of games planned. Tag and that sort of thing. But it was raining, so we couldn't go outside. We decided to play a game of hide-and-seek instead," he said.

At the words *hide-and-seek*, a small gasp escaped Casey's lips. Was that why she'd been dreaming about the game?

"Are you all right?" Mr. Anderson glanced over at her from beneath his bushy eyebrows.

"Yes, sorry," Casey said. "Please go on."

"Millie wanted to be It," Mr. Anderson told them. "But we wouldn't let her. *I* wouldn't let her. Millie had an uncanny way of knowing certain things that nobody else could know. I don't know how. But that day I told the other kids that I thought it would be unfair. So we made Anna Henriksson It instead. She was only about six years old at the time."

"Anna Henriksson is my grandmother," Erik told him.

Mr. Anderson nodded and looked down at his hands. Casey and Erik waited for him to continue.

"Well, Anna counted to twenty and we all hid. Anna wasn't much good at finding anyone, being so young, but eventually we all turned up — except Millie. We didn't think much of it at first. We assumed she was just trying to win the game. She could be stubborn that way.

"But then it was getting on toward dark, and she was still missing. We walked all over the property, calling her name. By now her folks were real worried. They called the sheriff over in Lincoln, and he put together a search party with hound dogs and everything. They combed the woods, but they never found her."

Casey tried to swallow and realized her mouth was dry. Her heart had started to beat faster.

"A week or so passed," Mr. Anderson went on. "One day Millie's mother went up in the attic to look for something. She opened a trunk . . . and there was Millie, all curled up like she was asleep. She'd hidden in there during our game. The lid closed tight on her, and she suffocated. She probably died while we were all out looking for her."

Casey covered her mouth with her hands. Erik looked down at his lap.

"Her funeral was the day before school started. She would have been in the eighth grade." Mr. Anderson paused and cleared his throat before he went on. "After that, we didn't see much of Millie's parents. I heard Mr. Hughes wanted to go back to Manchester, where they'd come from. But Millie's mother wouldn't leave the house. She claimed Millie was still there, and she didn't want to leave her behind. I suspect she was mad with grief." He shook his head. "I can't imagine what it would do to a parent, finding your child like that."

"Did you ever talk to them? Her parents?" Erik asked Mr. Anderson.

"We kids never spoke of it again to anyone," the man replied. "I think we all felt somewhat responsible. Anna Henriksson took it especially hard. She was just a little girl when it happened. She looked up to Millie. I think she felt that if she'd looked harder, she could have found her."

"But it wasn't Gran's fault. It wasn't anyone's fault," Erik said. "It was just an accident."

"I know. But . . ." Mr. Anderson spread his hands. "Sometimes things happen in your life that you wish you could go back and change. I can't help but think, if only we hadn't played hide-and-seek. If only I'd let her be It like she wanted, she might still be alive."

Slumped in his easy chair, Mr. Anderson looked small and frail. It was hard for Casey to imagine him as the smug, confident boy Millie had described in her diary.

"She looked a lot like you, you know," Mr. Anderson told her. "I'll see if I can find our class picture."

He got up stiffly and shuffled out of the room. After several minutes, he came back holding a black-and-white photograph. He handed it to Casey.

"This was taken the school year before she died," he said. "Millie is in the first row. The third one from the left."

The children were lined up in three rows. The girls wore dresses with little round collars, and the boys had on white shirts and ties, but otherwise they could have been Casey's schoolmates. Casey studied Millie's smiling face. The photo was faded, but she could tell that they had the same wavy black hair, the same stubborn mouth, the same dark, curious eyes.

"The first time I saw you, I thought I was looking at a ghost," Mr. Anderson said. "And then I heard you were living at the house on Drury Road. . . ."

Casey nodded. So that was why he had seemed so surprised and frightened.

She gave the picture back to him. "I think I have something that belongs to you." Reaching into her pocket, Casey pulled out the green-and-white marble. She placed it in his hand.

He looked at it for a long time. When he raised his eyes, Casey saw that they were damp. "She won this from me," he told Casey. "At the time, I thought she cheated."

"I know," Casey said. "She wrote about that, too."

The old man handed the marble back to her. "You keep it. I think Millie would want you to have it."

"Thank you," Casey said. "And thank you for telling us about Millie."

"Did you find out what you wanted to know?" he asked.

"Yes," Casey said. She had her answer, though she wasn't sure she was glad.

"Good. Well, feel free to visit anytime," he said. "I don't get many visitors these days."

"We will," Erik promised.

Casey and Erik got up to leave. At the door, Casey remembered something. "One more thing," she said to Mr. Anderson. "Do you know anything about a fire at Millie's old house?"

Mr. Anderson frowned. "A fire? No, I would have remembered that. There's never been a fire on Drury Road."

CHAPTER SIXTEEN

Casey and Erik made their way home slowly, walking their bikes so that they could talk.

"Poor Gran," Erik said. "That's why she never wanted us to talk about that old house. She probably felt sad about Millie her whole life, but she never said a word about it."

"Poor *Millie*. What a horrible way to die." Casey shuddered. "She dreamed about it, you know," she told Erik. "She dreamed she was in a dark place, calling for her parents. But she didn't know what it meant."

"That's horrible," Erik agreed. "But at least now you know you're safe. What happened to Millie was an accident. It won't happen again. It won't happen to *you*."

But how can I be sure of that? Casey thought. Obviously, she wouldn't go climbing into any old trunks — that was a no-brainer. But how did she know something else, something just as bad, wouldn't happen to her? She could go skipping down the lane and cut her foot on a rusty nail. Or she could be eating a simple, healthy dinner and suddenly choke to death on a chicken bone.

It hadn't been a ghost that killed Millie; it had been a simple game of hide-and-seek, and in a way that scared Casey even more. It didn't matter whether you took chances or not, she thought. Nothing was safe. You could hardly *live* for the fear of dying.

Casey didn't know how to explain all this to Erik. Instead, she said, "But that still doesn't explain what's been happening in the house — the broken vase and the cabinet that almost fell on me. Those weren't just accidents."

"Maybe it was Millie," he suggested. "You heard what Mr. Anderson said. Millie's mother thought she still lived in the house. Maybe she really did — or her spirit did, anyway."

Casey frowned. "But why would she do all those things? Why would she try to hurt us or scare us?"

"She could be angry," Erik replied. "Maybe she's jealous that you're alive and she's not."

Casey wondered if that could be true. Had Millie been behind all the frightening things that had happened?

It's hard to believe, she thought. *She felt so much like my friend.*

They had reached the dead-end sign. Casey and Erik both stopped and stared at the two words. They had suddenly taken on a new meaning.

Finally, Erik turned to Casey. She thought he was going to say good-bye. Instead, to her astonishment, he hugged her.

Casey was so surprised that it took her a moment to hug him back. When she finally did, she found she didn't want to let go.

"Are you going to be okay?" he asked when he released her.

"I don't know . . . I — I think so," Casey stuttered, feeling a little dazzled.

"I have to go home now," Erik told her. "But maybe I could come by tomorrow? To hang out, and, you know, keep the ghosts away?"

Casey smiled, feeling pleased and shy all at once. "That would be great."

Erik nodded. "Okay. See you then."

"See you."

He got on his bike and pedaled back down the road. Casey turned and walked slowly toward home, marveling at the strangeness of life. Sometimes, she thought, the things that started out frightening were the things that felt safest after all.

CHAPTER SEVENTEEN

For the rest of the afternoon, Casey felt a confusing mix of emotions. She felt sad and sickened whenever she thought about Millie and the terrible way she'd died. But thoughts of Erik kept creeping into her mind, pushing out the sadness. Each time she remembered hugging him, she felt a little thrill.

For the first time since she'd come to Stillness, Casey found herself looking forward to something. Tomorrow couldn't come soon enough.

By evening, she was still thinking about Erik. "I'm going nuts," Casey laughed at herself as she climbed into bed. "I'd better watch out or I'll dream about him, too."

But she didn't dream about Erik. That night, for the first time, Casey dreamed of Millie's fire. She smelled the harsh, acrid smoke and heard the ferocious crackling. It was just as Millie had described it in her diary. Casey even dreamed that she could hear Millie herself. She was shouting at Casey, *Get up! Get up! Get up!*

Casey opened her eyes. There was light outside her window, but it didn't look like sunrise. The air in her room smelled bitter. Casey sucked in a breath and started to choke.

She squeezed her eyes shut again. "It's just a dream," she told herself, digging her fingernails into her palms. "Wake up! Wake up!"

A loud crash made her jerk upright. Her room was awash in glowing light. Looking out the window, Casey could see that the porch, a floor beneath her, was on fire. Part of it had collapsed, sending orange flames shooting toward the sky.

She leaped up from the bed. *Dream or not,* she thought, *I have to get out of here.*

Smoke hung like a blanket over the room. It stung her eyes, blinding her. Casey moved forward slowly, arms outstretched, yelping as she tripped over a pair of sneakers she'd left in the middle of the floor.

At last she felt the edge of the door beneath her fingertips. It felt warm, and Casey knew the fire must be close. But she had to open it. The door was her only way out.

Using her T-shirt to protect her hand, Casey grasped the doorknob and pulled open the door. A wave of blistering heat washed over her.

The corridor was filled with flames. Beyond it, she could see more flames climbing up the stairs.

"Mom!" Casey screamed. "Dad!"

There was no answer. All she heard was the roar of the fire. She didn't know if her parents were trapped on the other side of the blaze, or if they'd somehow made it out of the house.

"Mom! Dad! Are you there? Help me!"

Bits of ash swirled around Casey's head like a blizzard. The flames reached toward her, hungry for the air in her room.

Casey slammed the door against them, and backed away. "Help me!" she screamed again, even though she knew no one could hear her.

Out of the corner of her eye, she saw something move. Casey spun around and came face-to-face with her reflection in the dressing table mirror. Through a haze of smoke and tears, she caught a glimpse of tangled black hair, a soot-smudged face. Her dark eyes were wide with terror.

Casey had a sickening sense of déjà vu. Then she realized why.

I read this, she thought. *This was in Millie's journal. She saw it all, every detail.*

But Millie had misunderstood one thing. The girl she had seen in the mirror, the one who'd been trapped in the fire — it wasn't Millie, after all. It was Casey.

The wallpaper around the door had started to blister, the printed ferns twisting and curling from the heat. Soon, Casey knew, the wall itself would be on fire. Then it would be only a matter of moments before the whole room was swallowed in flames.

Casey could barely breathe now. Smoke filled the room. Vaguely, she remembered from lessons at school that you were supposed to get low in a fire. On her hands and knees, she crawled as far away from the door as possible. When her hand struck a wall, she huddled against it.

From beyond the door there came a crash that made the floor shudder. Casey guessed it was the staircase giving way. She hoped at least her parents had made it out in time.

I'm going to die here, Casey thought. Dimly, she wondered if Millie had had the same thought before she died.

As she sat there with her head tucked into the crook of her elbow, Casey felt a hand grasp hers; solid, real fingers laced through her own. Someone was pulling her to her feet.

Mom? Casey thought. But it wasn't her mother's hand. Through her tears, Casey could barely make out the figure of a girl. The hand grasping hers felt small and strong.

Casey allowed herself to be pulled upward, toward the small far window, the one that had never opened.

The window! Casey thought. And suddenly, she realized there was still a way out.

Just then, the fingers holding her let go. Casey reached out blindly, desperate for the return of that

reassuring grip. But her fingers brushed against nothing. There was no one there.

But now she was on her feet and she knew she had a chance to save herself. She grabbed the bedside lamp and broke the window on the second try. Suddenly, she could hear her parents. They were somewhere on the ground, screaming in voices she'd never heard before. Voices full of panic.

Casey used the base of the lamp to knock the rest of the glass away from the frame and managed to get one leg out the window. The fire lit up the area bright as day, and she could see the ground clearly, a scraggly patch of dirt and weeds. It lurched before her eyes, and her heart seized up with fear.

"I can't do it!" she cried.

Yes you can, a voice said clearly. It came not from the room, but from somewhere within her mind, and Casey recognized it at once. It was the voice from her dreams. Millie's voice.

Behind Casey, there was a roar. The fire had eaten away the door and was spreading across the wall of her room.

Now, go! the voice said.

Casey looked down at the ground again. It

seemed to swim in the smoky haze. She closed her eyes against the sight. As she swung the other leg over the windowsill, Casey cried out, "Ready or not, here I come!"

Then she jumped.

CHAPTER EIGHTEEN

By the time the fire trucks arrived, most of the house had been destroyed. After they'd put it out, the firefighters guessed that the fire had started in the kitchen, then spread quickly to the dining room and up the stairs.

"An old wooden house like this is a tinderbox," the head fireman told Casey's parents. "You're lucky we had that storm the night before. If the wood had been dry, the fire would have spread even faster."

Casey shivered at the thought. Any faster and she wouldn't have made it out.

She leaned back against the side of the fire truck, pulling the blanket tighter around her shoulders.

Not long after the fire trucks had shown up, Erik and his mother and the twins had arrived with blankets and thermoses of coffee. Erik was the one who'd called the fire department. He'd spotted the blaze over the tops of the trees.

"Do you have any idea how it started?" Casey's dad asked. He was still in his pajamas, wrapped in a plaid blanket. In one hand, he held a thermos lid full of coffee, which he seemed to have forgotten about. He hadn't taken a single sip.

"Hard to say. Often in these old places the problem is electrical," the fireman said. "They've got old, frayed wires, sometimes with nothing but some rotten cloth for insulation. You plug in a few modern appliances — computers, coffeemakers, and whatnot — and, well, the worn-out wires just can't take the heat, if you pardon the expression."

"You think that's what it was, then? An electrical fire?" asked Casey's mother, who looked pale and shaken. She had both hands wrapped around a cup of coffee as if holding on to it for dear life.

"Could be," the fireman said. "Often there are clues. Lightbulbs flickering. Things shorting out. You folks have anything like that?"

Casey's father nodded. "We did have some flickering lights."

"Well, then," said the fireman. "Anyway, I expect the insurance company will do a full investigation. You had insurance on this place, didn't you?"

"Yes," said Casey's mother. "Thank goodness for that."

The fireman looked back toward the charred remains of the house, and Casey followed his gaze. The front portion was still standing. But the porch, the kitchen, Casey's room, and most of the attic were gone.

"Darn shame," the fireman said, shaking his head. "What I don't understand is living all the way out here without a phone. You're lucky this boy happened to see the fire, and had the presence of mind to call us." He patted Erik's shoulder with a gloved hand.

Erik just nodded, accepting the praise but not relishing it. As Casey's parents and the fireman continued to talk, Erik moved over to Casey's side. "How are you doing?" he asked.

"I'm okay," she said. The firemen had bandaged her sprained ankle and one of her hands, which she'd cut climbing through the broken window. Her eyes burned fiercely and her lungs still ached from the smoke. But she was alive.

Erik took Casey's good hand and gave it a gentle squeeze. Casey was startled. What was he thinking, holding her hand right in front of their parents?!

She started to pull away. Then she stopped. Erik's words from their afternoon at the stream suddenly echoed in her head: *What's the worst that could happen?*

Nothing, Casey thought. *Or nothing bad, anyway.* And instead of pulling her hand away, she squeezed back. Then she laughed.

"When you said you'd come by tomorrow, this wasn't exactly what I had in mind," she joked.

But Erik didn't laugh. He leaned toward Casey with a worried expression. "Do you think she did it?" he asked, lowering his voice. "Millie, I mean. Do you think she could have started the fire?"

Casey shook her head. "No, definitely not."

"How can you be sure?" asked Erik. "After the other things that happened. How do you know she didn't do this, too?"

Casey thought of Millie's voice, clear and firm, urging her, *Get up!* Millie had been the one to warn her that the fire had started. In fact, Casey realized, she had been warning her all along.

"She was trying to protect us," she said, thinking aloud. As she said it, she knew that it was true. "She knew what was going to happen, and she was trying to scare us out of the house, so no one got hurt. Only it didn't work."

She was like my guardian angel, Casey thought.

Erik's mother came over to them. She held one of the twins, who was asleep on her shoulder.

"You poor thing. You look exhausted," she said to Casey. "Why don't you all come over to our house and get some sleep?" she added, turning to Casey's parents. "Once you're rested, you can use the phone to make some calls."

"Thank you. That's very kind of you," Casey's mother replied. "We'll need to find a hotel to stay in until we can make arrangements with our subletters back in New York."

Back in New York. Casey felt a sudden pang. Of course they would be going back to New York, since they no longer had a house here. Why hadn't that occurred to her until this moment?

Suddenly, Casey wasn't ready to leave Stillness. Who knew if she would ever come back? And what if she never saw Erik again?

She looked into his face and realized he was thinking the same thing.

Calm down, Casey told herself. *You're going to be fine.* After all, she had just escaped a fire, jumped from a second-floor window, and held hands with a boy right in front of everyone. In the last twelve hours, Casey had surprised herself more than she ever had in her entire life. It seemed like this new obstacle was probably something that she could deal with.

The sun was just starting to rise as Casey's parents helped her into the backseat of the car. Casey rolled down the window and leaned out, looking back at the house one last time. She was hoping she would see some sign of Millie.

But there was nothing. In the cold, morning light, the remains of the house looked utterly empty. The house was gone, and, Casey thought, so was Millie.

"Thank you," she whispered, anyway, just in case.

Casey watched the house until they turned around the bend and it disappeared from sight. Then she turned to face forward, ready for whatever came next.

BITE INTO THE NEXT POISON APPLE, IF YOU DARE. . .

Over a delicious dinner of perfectly cooked hamburgers, Great-aunt Margo talked about her hometown in Romania. A small village with a funny name, it was nestled deep in the Carpathian Mountains, and it sounded beautiful. Margo described lush green forests, clear blue streams, narrow cobblestone streets, and ancient castles.

As she spoke — and Mom chimed in with memories of photographs her parents had shown her — I glanced out the window at the Manhattan skyline. Though I loved the tall buildings and concrete sidewalks of New York City, I liked the idea of such a rural, quaint place . . . the place my ancestors had lived! Suddenly, I realized that Great-aunt Margo had given me a great starting point for my social studies project.

Excited, I helped with the dishes and excused myself for the night. Then I headed into my room, grabbed my laptop, and sat cross-legged on my bed.

I opened Google, then typed in the name of my family's Romanian village, grateful for the *Did you mean?* feature after I'd misspelled it twice. Then I clicked on the Wikipedia page; it showed a pretty picture of the forests Great-aunt Margo had talked about, and gave the basic facts: population, map coordinates, and weather. Then, as I skimmed the page, I spotted a sentence that made my jaw drop.

Located in the region once known as Transylvania, this small town is still home to many vampire legends.

I sat back, my pulse racing. *Transylvania*? As in, Count Dracula territory? I had no idea that my family came from *there*. Intrigued, I started to read more, but then my IM pinged. It was Gabby.

Bad news! she'd written. Dentist said I have to get braces! ☹

I was still preoccupied by the whole Transylvania thing, but I tried to turn my attention to my best friend.

That totally bites! I typed back, hoping to make her smile.

Her response popped up immediately: Am so not LOL-ing. Of course u can joke about it, Em. U have perfect teeth!

I shook my head. Though my dentist had recently declared that I wouldn't need braces (I'd celebrated with a candy feast that had resulted in three cavities), my teeth were *far* from perfect. I rose up on my knees so I was facing the mirror above my dresser, and I opened my mouth in an exaggerated smile. There they were, in the corners of my mouth — my super-embarrassing, super-pointy teeth. My dentist called them "incisors" and had even remarked that mine were sharper than most. I knew he was being nice by not calling them what they really were: fangs.

I heard another *ping!* and glanced back at my computer.

And ur "fangs" don't count! Gabby had written.

She seemed upset, so I decided to call her. By the time we said good-bye, it was late, so I finished the Edgar Allan Poe story I had to read for English, brushed my imperfect teeth, changed into my pj's, and crawled into bed.

As usual, I crawled into bed but I couldn't sleep.

First, I flipped onto my side, then my belly, then my back. Passing headlights from cars threw strange shapes onto my ceiling. The falling raindrops sounded like fingertips tapping against my windowpane. Then I remembered the Wikipedia page I'd stopped reading, and I sat up.

Without turning on the light, I eased out of bed and walked over to my desk. Sinking into my chair, I opened my laptop, and went back to where I had left off:

Located in the region once known as Transylvania, this small town is still home to many vampire legends. one such legend is about a certain breed of vampires who can shape-shift into bats, which then feast upon human and animal blood. In ancient times, villagers became so fearful that they hung knobs of garlic from their doorways, as it was said that the scent warded off the fanged creatures.

BANG!

The loud sound made me jump up so fast that I almost knocked over my chair. The bang hadn't been a clap of thunder, or one of the many sirens I was used to hearing at all hours. It hadn't even come from outside. It had come from right next door.

From the guest room.

Maybe Great-aunt Margo, like me, had trouble sleeping. Maybe she was unpacking, and the two of us could have a midnight snack. Maybe we could even discuss the vampire legends of her town. I was curious to learn more. For someone who enjoyed horror stories, I knew very little about vampires.

I tiptoed into the hallway. A window was open somewhere in the apartment, and I shivered in my thin pajamas. As my eyes adjusted to the darkness, I saw that the door to the guest room was ajar.

Moving as silently as possible, I crept over and paused on the threshold. The long, narrow room was blanketed in darkness, and the one window at its far end was open. The damp breeze lifted the gauzy white curtains, making them dance like restless ghosts. Piles of fancy-looking luggage were in the center of the room, and the scent of Great-aunt Margo's perfume filled the air. But Margo herself was nowhere to be found. The bed was still neatly made, and the room was empty.

Except for the cages and cages full of bats.

Stuffed bats, I reminded myself as I stepped inside.

I was still getting used to the fact that Great-aunt Margo was Romania's leading expert on vampire bats. She seemed like someone who'd have a more glamorous job. I held my breath, spooked by the sight of the dark, silent creatures. They all hung upside down from the bars of the cages, their leathery wings tucked against their furry bodies and their beady eyes shut tight. *Like they're sleeping*, I thought, shuddering.

Great-aunt Margo was even weirder than I'd thought! Did she put her stuffed bats into these poses every night, as if they were her dolls or pets or something? And where *was* she? She couldn't have gone outside in the rain. Was she in the kitchen?

Before I could turn to leave the room, lightning flashed outside, and I gave a start. For a second, the bat cage nearest me was lit up, and I saw that the cage door was swinging wide open. That must have been the bang I'd heard earlier: the wind blowing open the cage. I leaned over to close the small door.

Suddenly, one of the bats inside opened its eyes.

Its tiny, bright red eyes.